Murder in China

By Charlotte Epstein

MURDER IN CHINA

Murder in China

CHARLOTTE EPSTEIN

A CRIME CLUB BOOK
DOUBLEDAY
NEW YORK   LONDON   TORONTO   SYDNEY   AUCKLAND

A Crime Club Book
Published by Doubleday, a division of
Bantam Doubleday Dell Publishing Group, Inc.
666 Fifth Avenue, New York, New York 10103

Doubleday and the portrayal of a man
with a gun are trademarks of
Doubleday, a division of Bantam Doubleday Dell
Publishing Group, Inc.

Library of Congress Cataloging-in-Publication Data
Epstein, Charlotte.
Murder in China / Charlotte Epstein.
p. cm.
I. Title.
"A Crime Club Book"
PS3555.P645M87 1989
813'.54—dc19 89-30922
CIP

ISBN 0-385-26197-7

Murder in China

Xing Qi Wu—Friday

1

Janet woke in the dark, hearing angry voices in the corridor of the Foreign Students Building, a loud click and the sound of a door shutting. One of the voices went on and on, getting louder and then fading to a mutter—and silence. Her bedside clock read three and she turned on her side and fell asleep again.

She opened her eyes to the slap of the old doorman's slippers down the stone floor of the corridor, the scrape of metal on the stone as he emptied the wastebasket outside each door. There went the bugle over the p.a. system playing "My Old Kentucky Home." Now the news, a pep talk on one of the Four Modernizations, and a stern lecture on littering. Although it was all in Chinese, she could understand some of it from the tone and the occasional familiar word.

She shivered. It was fantastically unbelievable to stand on the Great Wall at two in the afternoon, and poking around on the site of Peking Man was so exciting she could hardly breathe, but at six o'clock on an October morning it was just cold.

Well, there was nothing for it but to get out. She threw back the brocade quilt, grabbed her warm robe and toothbrush, and turned the door key in the lock very slowly so that it wouldn't open with a loud snap and wake Sally in the next room. It snapped anyhow, echoing like a shot. Then she remembered that Sally was missing, and the worry started again.

She made her way to the bathroom to turn on the shower and let it run, hoping against hope that the water would get hot. Ten minutes exactly to brush her teeth and shower before the rush began. The Chinese women came only to use the toilet and throw some cold water on their faces. She grinned: They showered together in the late afternoons—two at a time in the single stall, laughing and giggling and talking away, steaming up the bathroom for hours. She had no idea when Sally showered. Where *was* the child?

"Damn!" she muttered, and stomped out to get the soap she had forgotten. Incredibly, for this early in the morning, Colette was knocking at her door. She was wearing the same loose, cassocklike dress she had been wearing to breakfast for weeks. Her curly black hair, even uncombed, was beautiful and her skin pale, unflawed ivory.

"What's the matter?" Janet asked.

Sally opened her door and stared, her mouth characteristically open.

"Sally! Where've you been?"

"Huh?"

The look on Colette's face was part terror, part relish. "Someone has been murdered!" she whispered in French. "It is the old woman, I think. Li Mei Ling."

"Sally, are you all right?"

"I'm all right. What happened?"

"Don't you know that everybody's been frantic about you?"

"Huh?" she said again.

Janet shook her head to clear it and decided to put all discussions off until later. "Forgot the soap," she mumbled.

"Janet!" Colette seized her arm. "You 'ave 'eard what 'appens?"

"Colette," she said sweetly, patting the Frenchwoman's cheek, "it's six o'clock in the morning and I can't cope without lipstick. Tell me later, okay?"

Colette grabbed her own hair with both hands and spoke rapidly in French again. Histrionics for a change.

"What did you say?"

"*La vieille*—the old woman—Li . . . !"

Janet pouted. Sixty was hardly old, she thought, conscious of her own fifty years.

". . . *elle est morte!*"

"What? Did you say she was dead?"

"Yes. Dead. Murdered, I think."

"Murdered!" The three women stared at each other as the word echoed around them.

Janet pulled her robe closer. "Don't be silly, Colette. I left the shower running. I have to teach this morning." And she started back to the bathroom. Murder. Not possible. That young woman makes a three-act melodrama out of every rumor. I wonder if something has really happened to Mrs. Li.

An overwhelming curiosity was Janet Eldine's prevailing trait. It had taken her to Australia, New Zealand, Alaska, and half a dozen other places to discover how the people in different cultures responded to a variety of social facts like population diversity and physical disability. But she wasn't interested in Colette's announcement. She told herself that it was just one more in a series of doom-and-gloom bulletins that never turned out to be anything more than rumor or wish. She hoped that her bump of curiosity would not be permanently flattened by her exposure to Colette.

"I'll be right out," she called over her shoulder. "Don't solve the murder without me."

Colette stared after her and grunted in frustration. "That one, she would be on time for work if there were a second revolution! I tell you, the old woman has been murdered! I must go. My head aches and I have preparations to make for my teacher. I will speak to you later." And she was gone—to a busy day of Chinese lessons and discussions of ancient Chinese history. She was one of the few visiting scholars in China, and certainly one of the very few people outside the country who read classical Chinese. She was working on some obscure period of Chinese history she seemed never to have the patience to talk about. But nothing would be permitted to interfere with the work on her dissertation.

Sally shrugged. She got her toothbrush and walked down to the bathroom, forgetting the unspoken agreement between Janet and herself that they would not intrude on each other.

Janet tossed her robe over the stall door and tripped in the over-size plastic sandals all foreigners were instructed to wear. She soaped herself energetically to neutralize the cold water and sang, careful not to get any water in her mouth. No one drank the water in China without boiling it first. The sheer excitement of being in China welled up in her, as it had every day for a month since her arrival at the college, Beijing Xue Yuan. Nothing could spoil it for her—not foreign experts' paranoia, not the daily small physical discomforts, and definitely not Mrs. Li.

She had come from the college of education of a large urban university that was suffering from the throes of falling enrollments and bad management. Fed up with the bickering and backbiting among a faculty scared out of its wits at the threats of retrenchment and loss of tenure, she had jumped at the chance offered her by a Chinese scientist who told her that his engineering college in Beijing was looking for an American to teach English to scientists. The small college, administered by the Ministry of Education, called up scientists from around the country to prepare them for going abroad to do advanced research.

"Would you be interested?" the visiting scientist had asked her.

"Make me an offer," she had quipped, meaning only that her job was getting her down. And he had made her an offer.

In less than three weeks her leave of absence was signed, her furniture was in storage, and her brother was handing her a new Polaroid camera at the airport. She must remember to ask him to send film. No Polaroid film was available in China.

In that time, she had researched the methods of teaching English as a foreign language, collected books and teaching materials to take with her, and developed a detailed teaching plan. She hadn't felt so keyed up about work since the retrenchments had begun! And China—she was really in China!

2

Sally reached the door as Janet was coming out of the bathroom. From where they stood they could see the building lobby. The old doorman stood with two younger men, all three talking excitedly.

"Apparently something *has* happened. Was Colette right?"

"It's about Mrs. Li all right. Outside. He saw something outside, I think," said Sally. "I can only make out a word here and there." She listened again, breathing through her mouth. "No." She shook her head. "They're talking too fast for me. I can't get it."

Chang, the odd character who always hung on the fringes of any two foreigners who were speaking English, came toward them, gearing up to use his limited English—limited but distinguishing in the Foreign Students Building, where none of the other workers spoke English. "Something bad." He smiled inappropriately. "Mrs. Li. Uh . . . uh." He pantomimed, holding his hands around his own throat and sticking his tongue out. He eyes bulged and his face got red.

"Strangled?"

He smiled more widely. "Police come. Soldiers come." He nodded emphatically.

"Where? Where did it happen?" Robbery? This building was so carefully guarded against Chinese visitors, but anyone could get in easily through the ground-level windows.

"Outside. Back."

She remembered being wakened at three in the morning. Had she heard something happening to Mrs. Li? A peremptory bark from the old man called Chang away. He didn't approve of fraternizing with foreigners.

"We'd better finish dressing and then try to get something to eat before class." But she didn't move. She thought of Mrs. Li, the small, nut-brown woman, stepping quickly through the halls of the building. Although her face was wrinkled, her shoe-button eyes were snappingly clear and her step firm. And she talked incessantly from morning until night—a real Chinese yenta.

"Do you think it's true, that she was murdered?" asked Sally.

"Not just for talking."

"Huh?"

"Nothing. A lot of people didn't like her very much."

Janet herself had complained about the endless plates of soggy cabbage and dry tough hunks of pork, about the dirty floors and bathroom basins caked with old soap. Although she felt the complaints were justified, she worried about what she had begun to feel was her constant carping. Once, in the dining room, she had watched a Japanese visitor. Every time a waiter made a mistake or the assistant cook hawked and almost spat, every time he saw something that was not quite right, he made a disgusted face, indicating to the other foreigners his contempt for the Chinese. And all the time he sat there, Janet noticed that his fly was open. She sometimes wondered if she was sitting there with her fly open.

In spite of everything, the American professor had to admire the old-guard Chinese revolutionary whose beliefs and actions were so firmly grounded in principle. The fact that her cherished principles had in large part been abandoned by the current government must have baffled and enraged Mrs. Li. Janet could even feel some pity for her, having to continue fighting the old war against increasing odds.

3

The staff were all in the dining room. At the counter by the kitchen, breakfast was being dispensed by the pleasant-faced, middle-aged woman: a hard-boiled egg—cold—if you wanted it, cold toast if you could get it down, tea that must have been standing all night. Only when there was some kind of regional meeting in the building did the cook make *yo bing,* the delicious fried pastry that reminded Janet of Pennsylvania Dutch funnel cake. Sally had the gruel of rice and hot water that most of the Chinese people had for breakfast. Sliced cold pork from last night's dinner was available.

The short, fat cook, in his incredibly dirty apron with a cigarette dangling from his mouth, held court at one of the round tables. Two young men, a young girl, and a very old assistant cook sat with him, their animated talk ceasing abruptly for his occasional comment. Every once in a while the assistant cook would clear his throat with the hawking sound that disgusted foreigners. Mercifully, the dining room staff had been warned not to spit on the floor.

Two of the African students stumbled in, rubbing the sleep from their eyes. A third, Ka Ka Chi, walked in, beautifully groomed as usual, ready for the day's classes. He brought his hard-boiled egg to the table and grinned at Sally. "So, you have returned. There has been much worry for you."

Sally just frowned. A college junior who had taken a year off when a Chinese exchange student at her college had urged her to apply for the job at Beijing Xue Yuan, she was supposed to have conversation in English with students while Janet provided more systematic instruction in the language. But she really didn't care if the students never learned English, and she barely made contact with her fellow residents in the Foreign Students Building. She had just wanted a few months in China, away from school and her family. She reminded Janet of many of the students at home—uneducated and uninvolved.

"Good morning, madame," Ka Ka Chi greeted Janet. "Have you learned to speak Chinese yet?"

Janet laughed and made a face at him. What had taken him two years of intensive study at the Beijing Foreign Language Institute the American professor should be able to learn in two weeks.

"In another week I won't need your help. But right now . . ." She motioned to the round table. "Can you hear what they're saying?"

He listened for a moment and turned a half-surprised, half-amused look on her. "They talk about the old one—Li. They say she is killed. The old man found her in the back. She had a knife in her—a kitchen knife. Hah! Things will not be so good for them now, I think!"

"A knife? I thought she was strangled."

He shrugged. "They say a knife."

"Do they have any idea who could have done it?"

"One says a thief, perhaps. The cook, he disagrees, but he does not say who. The security police have been called." He gulped the last of the tea in his cup and jumped to his feet. "It is time to go. My class is at eight today."

He walked quickly from the room. The other two students, suddenly wide awake, left their half-eaten breakfasts and followed him out—to classes in electrical engineering, hydraulics, systems design. One said something very low to the other, in Swahili, she thought.

They were conscientious students, sent as teenagers by their governments to study the engineering sciences so that they might contribute to their countries' development. Janet had become very friendly with Ka Ka Chi, from Zaire, who spoke excellent English and French. She could communicate also with Petiri, who came from Chad and spoke English. With most of the others she just exchanged casual greetings. Masomakali, the tall Nigerian who was under the impression that she could understand his dialect French and mangled English, was the most interesting of them all. He intruded himself into the life of everyone in the Foreign Students Building, not always with happy results.

With her translator gone, Janet finished the rocklike toast and the last of the spoonful of *guo jian*— a sort of apple marmalade—took a sip of the corrosive cold tea, and rose from the table. "I'm going out back to see what's happening. Want to come?" she asked Sally.

"Okay."

She won't express any qualms if I don't, Janet thought. Her own qualms were making her heart pound. But curiosity won.

Just inside the entrance to the building the old doorman and the two younger workers still sounded excited. Sally and Janet walked past them and out of the door into the bright sunshine of the quiet courtyard. The small planting in the middle had already been watered. Already, too, laundry dripped from the wires strung between trees at the far perimeter of the court. Janet did a double take at the laundry and recognized her own panty hose and bras. Well, she was grateful she didn't have to launder them herself, although she would prefer not to have them decorating the court. A fleeting vision of her underwear strung across the quad of her own university almost made her giggle.

The two women turned left out of the large wooden gate in the wall that surrounded the Foreign Students Building. The paved path leading to the back of the building was bordered with four-foot-high stacks of bricks and piles of sand. A wheelbarrow blocked the end of the path. They stepped around it into soft, damp sand up to their ankles.

"Ugh, what a mess! Where are the workmen?"

"There they are." Sally pointed through the glassless window spaces of the half-finished structure. They could see through to the back of it where several people in their faded blue cotton pants and white shirts sat on wooden planks on the ground talking. Janet looked around, undecided, and jerked convulsively. Not ten feet away from them, half covered by a small mound of sand, lay what looked at first like a discarded pair of blue pants and white shirt. As she stared, the objects sorted themselves out into a person, lying as if tossed against the sand by a strong wind. The right arm was flung up, fingers half curled on an open palm. The other arm was stretched out to the side, also palm up. The body was turned slightly on its side, as if the weight of the fall had been taken by the right side. Only part of the left side of the face could be seen. The short, straight hair had fallen over it, covering the forehead and part of the left eye.

"God," Janet whispered. "It *is* Mrs. Li."

No one watched the site. There might have been footprints earlier but now the sand was just smudged about, with no way of telling anything useful. She looked up at the five stories of another one of those brick, flat-roofed blocks that were going up everywhere in Beijing. This building was in the ugliest of Western tradition, another slum tenement in the making. What a shame they could not, even in their rush to provide desperately needed housing, find some way to keep even a few of the beautiful architectural details from the past: a fluted green roof, a mosaic trim, or an occasional painted column.

"Ni zuo shenmo?"

She jumped. A young man in wrinkled khaki stood there trying to look stern. She recognized the uniform of the People's Liberation Army that identified soldiers. The security police who investigated serious crimes were a unit of the army.

"He asks what you are doing," said Colette, coming up the path.

"Yes, I understood that." She wished Colette hadn't come; she might have tried to answer in Chinese. "Tell him I'm just looking. Say I live here and I wonder who did this terrible thing."

The soldier said something in reply that she couldn't understand. Although he didn't smile, she could see "the look" on his face. The look was a mixture of curiosity about foreigners, with whom the Chinese had so little contact; the natural friendliness and exuberance of the Chinese people; and the xenophobic mistrust, a tradition that was fostered by memories of the persecution of imperialist running dogs during the Cultural Revolution and the current government admonitions not to get too close to the representatives of Western decadence.

"He wants to know where we are from," Colette said. "They're American; I'm French." She tried to smile as she gave him this information.

"American!" He turned to Janet and Sally. Americans were irresistible. "Hello," he said.

Janet smiled. "Hello."

His only English word, probably. The teenagers shouted it as she window-shopped among the crowds on Wangfujing.

"Why are you so nervous? You're not the only one who fought with Mrs. Li."

"I do not trust this PLA! They do as they please."

"Oh, really. There are laws." Even as she said it, she thought: How American! She knew very well that the law here was pretty much what those in authority in a situation said it was. A recent article in the *China Daily* mentioned the plans for developing a legal code. If it was ever done it might make the security police a little less terrifying.

Mrs. Hua was inside the entrance, talking softly to a soldier, smiling up into his face. Janet called Mrs. Hua "the Fixer." Whenever there was a problem with the foreigners, the college administration trotted out the Fixer—a charming woman who spoke English and French fluently, and gamely tackled any problem, but never succeeded in fixing anything.

"Ah, Dr. Aldane! You are here!" Janet's name was Eldine, but this was the closest most people could get to the pronunciation.

"Hello, Mrs. Hua. Isn't it terrible about Mrs. Li?" Banalities filled in the gaps in understanding language and culture.

"Yes, terrible." The charming smile didn't quite leave her face. "There are questions the police must ask. You do not mind?"

"Mind? Of course not. But I don't know anything."

"It will take only a moment. Of course you are not involved."

She spoke only to Janet. Colette and Sally were in another social class—the first studying in China at her own request; the other merely young. "Perhaps we can sit in the dining room, yes? Everyone has finished eating."

When they came through the swinging door the cook and one of his helpers sprang apart. Their filthy aprons remained down, covering their blue cotton pants and white undershirts. They seemed to have forgotten the etiquette that required them to roll up the front of their aprons when they came out of the kitchen, to remove from sight the filth or the mark of servitude. In either case the dining-room workers who walked through the eating area did so with their arms wrapped in their rolled-up aprons, looking faintly abashed.

The cook had lost his habitual sneer and was sweating. The young one, no older than a junior high school boy with his bright eyes and eager friendliness, also looked frightened. They moved slowly backward as the four women and the soldiers came into the room, until they stood with their backs at the far wall. One officer stared impassively at them over the women's heads. Finally he motioned for Janet to sit. The others remained standing, watching the cook and his helper disappear into the kitchen.

Why were they so terrified? Had they had something to do with

Mrs. Li's death? Janet would have said that the cook was quite capable of murder. But now, looking at him turn green and cringe into the wall, she couldn't even believe she had ever seen him swat flies with such great satisfaction.

She remembered one day last week when there was shouting in the courtyard and she peeked through the gap in the curtains to see the cook and Mrs. Li yelling at each other. She had passed them on her way in and they had been speaking quietly, probably congratulating one another on how much of the food money they were managing to save by starving the foreigners. The conversation had heated up, but only for a moment, until they realized that people had turned to look at them. Their voices lowered again and the conversation went on. But it no longer looked amicable.

Chang was hanging out his washing. He had heard the yelling too and had been so entranced by what he had heard that he was still staring openmouthed at the two of them. Maybe Mrs. Li had threatened to expose something illegal that the cook was involved in. She would have considered any crime a blow against the revolution.

A yell sent the PLA man dashing toward the kitchen, but before he could open the door, the scene was framed by the opening at the counter. The cook was brandishing a cleaver at Chang, who was turning to run. He got out the back door before the policeman could intervene. There was a quick exchange between the policeman and the cook and the frame was empty again.

Mrs. Hua translated: Chang had just been acting in his usual annoying manner, getting in the way of people trying to get their work done. The cook had chased him away as he was forced to do regularly. The young soldier's wide grin as he explained to the man in charge made it clear that he thought it was nothing important.

4

The soldier seated the others at the table, then took his stand behind Mrs. Hua, from where he could see his superior's face. The officer spoke at some length and finally Mrs. Hua turned to Janet:

"Li Mei Ling has been slain. She was an honored soldier of the revolution and a valued cadre of her unit. The traitor who did this thing must be found and punished. We will find her and the people will decide what will be done with her.''

"Her? Why do you say her?'' Colette trembled visibly.

"No, no,'' Mrs. Hua said gently, smiling. "He says *ta*. You know that means her or him.''

"I know nothing, nothing. I feel very sick. I must go to my room.''

"It will be just a moment, Colette. Then you can go.''

"No! I must go now!'' She jumped to her feet and ran. The man who was standing suddenly came alive and started after her, but the other said something curtly that made him stop and return to the table.

Mrs. Hua made soothing sounds to the officer and Janet caught a word here and there. She was assuring him that Colette would be in her room and he would be able to talk to her later—presumably when she had calmed down. The officer nodded brusquely and rapped out a question at Janet.

"He asks if you saw Mrs. Li yesterday,'' Mrs. Hua said softly.

"Yesterday? I suppose so. She was here every day, wasn't she? Do they know how she was killed?''

"He says she was . . . uh . . . with a knife in her right side, up to the heart.'' Her smile vanished. "Also someone choked her.''

"What kind of knife was she stabbed with?''

"The cook's knife. From the kitchen. He says *he* asks the questions and you must answer.''

"Of course. Tell him I'm sorry. But I'm very interested. Tell him I'm a psychologist with some experience in police work.''

"He wants to know what time you saw Mrs. Li last.''

"What time? I don't think I can recall. . . . Oh, wait. Yes, I went into the office yesterday just before dinner to get meal tickets. That was about four-thirty. She was talking to the two women, and when I came in she walked out.''

"Did you speak to her?''

"No, we were not friendly since she put up a sign saying there would be hot water only from three to five in the afternoon.''

It had been unreasonable of her. Janet could understand the need to economize; institutions around the world never had enough money. But why not make the amenities equally available to everyone? Now there would be plenty of hot water for the workers in the building and their friends who lived in the compound, but the others would have to do without.

"Yes," said Mrs. Hua. "We tried to tell her. She wanted to save money." She glanced at the soldier. "It was for the good of the unit."

Janet's eyebrows went up. Not only Mrs. Hua but other faculty—and Janet's students—had said quite openly that Mrs. Li did not like foreigners and was not above trying to make things uncomfortable for them. Janet shook her head in resignation.

The look on her face must have communicated something, because the officer asked Mrs. Hua a question.

Well, he'd caught that. I didn't like her, that's for sure!

Mrs. Hua's soothing voice smoothed over the dislike. "He asks where you were at five o'clock yesterday afternoon." She seemed to be apologizing for the question.

"Right here in my room, getting ready for dinner." That was one thing in her life that had certainly changed. The Chinese were early to dinner, early to bed, and early to rise. Here in a suburb twenty miles from the center of Beijing there was nothing to do after dinner, especially when the summer was over. It wasn't a large institution like Beijing University, where there were always special lectures and entertainments for students and other residents. An occasional game of Scrabble with Sally or a glass of wine and a difficult chat with one of the African students was about the extent of the social life in the college compound. They did show movies once in a while, and on rare festival days the students danced to what sounded like ancient marches.

Groups of undergraduates had begun to wander over to practice their English with her, but the doorman, probably at the command of Mrs. Li, had barred them from the building. Most of them obeyed, and now in the evenings she met with the undergraduates outside the building. She sat and they stood. But it would be getting cold soon and they would have to find someplace indoors or discontinue the meetings.

"You met with some students after dinner yesterday?"

"Yes. That was about six-thirty."

"Mr. Xu was with you?"

She looked at him, surprised. Why did he single out Mr. Xu? "He came along about a quarter to seven and left in a few minutes. He has things to do at home."

"Did you see where Mr. Xu went when he left?"

"Yes, he went out the gate and continued down the road toward his home."

"You are certain of this?"

"I watched him leave. I was sorry to see him go so soon."

Poor Xu. She had the feeling, though he never said so, that his wife left all the housework to him. Sometimes he came in the evening with his two small daughters—lovely children, so shiny and bright and clean. Different from the way he looked, with his grayish undershirt full of holes and his gray cotton pants that looked, somehow, more wrinkled and loose than the pants of other Chinese.

"He knew Mrs. Li well," the officer said. "He worked in the countryside during the Gang of Four. She was there too."

Janet said nothing. She had no wish to reveal to the soldier that Mr. Xu had told her in great detail about his experiences during the Cultural Revolution. It was bad enough that he seemed to be linking the persecution of Xu with Mrs. Li.

Janet had got to know Mr. Xu rather well. He had rewired the electric heater in her room and she helped him write letters of application for advanced study in American universities. It was not unusual for him to appear at her door at eight in the morning. "I have a letter from a university. I do not understand it. You will help me, please?" There had been a delay in processing his application, or a form had been lost. She helped straighten it out.

"It's too bad it has to take so long," she told him. "But there's no way around it. In the meantime, I'm sure you are enjoying the extra time you have to spend with your family."

"Yes."

"You have two lovely children. You must be very proud of them."

"The older one is going to be an aviation engineer."

"Really? She has already decided?" The girl was about eleven years old.

"I decide. She will work in Beijing."

"Why is it so important for her to work in Beijing?"

"When I am old, she must care for me."

"Do you mean that you chose her vocation so that she'll be able to care for you in your old age?"

"Yes, it is necessary. If I had a son he would do it. But I have no son."

"What does it matter? Your daughters love you very much. I'm sure they'll see that you are cared for in your old age."

"A man must have a son." He smiled sadly. "It is very bad not to have a son."

"But you have two beautiful daughters! You've told me that you're very proud of them."

He said nothing, torn between a father's love and pride and the Chinese need to deny their own worth.

"What could a son be to you that your daughters cannot?"

"A man must have a son," he repeated.

She gave up. Even the United States, despite the rising awareness of a vigorous women's movement, had not been able to rid itself of this shibboleth. A boy to assert the father's masculinity—as if just any baby were not proof enough of that. A boy to carry on the family name—even if the family name no longer derived only from the father. A son and heir—even when there wasn't a dime in the bank.

"A son takes care of parents when they are old," Mr. Xu continued his argument.

Hah! she thought. I'd like a count of the number of daughters who assume responsibility for aged parents! "You think your daughters would not care for you if you were old and helpless?"

"I think they would care for me." He smiled complacently. But, she saw in his eyes, a son was still a son.

5

Mrs. Hua's voice brought her back to the present. "He wishes to know if you heard anything unusual outside your window. Between the time you came to your room and the time you left for dinner."

"No."

"He says Mrs. Li's daughter and her husband come to your class. He asks if you know them."

"Yes, of course. Yue Zhen and Mr. Guo."

"Did you see them here yesterday evening?"

It was not a bad idea to look into the movements of the victim's family. Most murders were committed by people who loved one another. She frowned in the effort to remember. "I think Mr. Guo was around but I don't think his wife was. No, I didn't see her."

After a brief exchange, Mrs. Hua shrugged. "He says he will speak to them. He . . ." The officer interrupted—at some length this time. Mrs. Hua seemed to remonstrate with him, very gently. He looked angry. His head jerked in Janet's direction and Mrs. Hua's eyes slid toward her too, and quickly away. What were they arguing about? What were they saying about her? Mrs. Hua's voice faded out and for a long moment there was silence. Neither of them looked at her.

"What is it? What did he say about me?"

"No, no, it is nothing." Mrs. Hua's eyes would not meet hers.

"Mrs. Hua! I have a right to know what he's saying about me! Just because I can't understand Chinese is no reason to keep me in the dark! I insist that you tell me!"

Mrs. Hua looked at the soldier. Something passed between them —and was there the faintest suggestion of a nod? "I am sorry," she murmured.

"Sorry? About what?"

"He has been told something. Perhaps it is trouble for you. But I do not think so," she added firmly.

Janet admired her courage, but then was instantly worried about herself. "What trouble?" she demanded.

"It is about the students. You . . . you . . ."

What the hell had she done? She was feeling guilty and didn't know why. And then, for a flashing instant, she did know why. The face of Wang Qu Qing, a junior in the college, flickered between her and Mrs. Hua. She liked the boy. He hung around the Foreign Students Building in spite of the demands of college officials and other cadres that he stay away from the foreigners.

"The . . . the young people. They are impatient. They do not remember the . . . They want so much . . ." The soldier slapped the table and made both women jump. Mrs. Hua spoke more quickly. "You tell the students much about the United States and they speak to you. They are not satisfied with China. Your talk makes them impatient."

Janet gasped. They were saying that she was trying to talk the students into rebellion! The Chinese government was forever warning about this—decadent foreigners who could corrupt their peo-

ple, who were not to be trusted. "Of course I talk about the United
States! Did you expect me to teach English without mentioning
America?" She felt breathless, outraged.

"No, no. It is only one or two people who speak of such things.
You are a good teacher, and we are grateful to you for teaching the
students."

Janet calmed down as quickly as she had exploded. "I'm sorry. It's
not your fault and I'm yelling at you, Mrs. Hua. There are reaction-
aries in my university too. Please forgive me."

"It is nothing, Dr. Aldane. Please. It is nothing."

Janet took a long breath and tried bravado. "I don't know what all
this has to do with murder. Will you ask him if there's anything else
he wants me for?"

Again a lengthy exchange. Then: "He says one of the cook's
helpers saw you walking from the back last night. He says you must
have seen Mrs. Li but you said nothing."

So much for bravado. She'd be lucky if she didn't end up in jail.

"Tell him I did walk that way. It's a shortcut from Building No. 3. I
go to visit a friend there. But I saw nothing. If he'll come back with
me I'll show him."

They followed her out. She noticed that the cook had appeared
quietly and was standing within earshot. He came out too. Apparently he did not have so much work to do that he could not stop to
eavesdrop on the interrogation.

"You see." She pointed. "I walked through the side gate and
along the finished pavement in front of the new building. The pile of
sand was between me and Mrs. Li. I couldn't have seen her even if
she was there at the time."

The officer listened to Mrs. Hua, giving no sign that he understood or accepted the explanation. Then he said something and
Mrs. Hua looked very surprised. "He asks me if you think you know
who killed Mrs. Li."

"He does? Well, my goodness! Does this mean he's satisfied that *I*
didn't do it?"

"He says if you are uh . . . uh . . . psychologist and you know
about people you will tell him what you know."

"Does he know what time she was murdered?"

"Sometime during last night. Perhaps very early in the night."

"Who found her?"

"The old doorman. He walks in the morning, very early. He finds her as it is getting light. They think perhaps the old man is not telling the truth. Just before dinner, he went to the dining room where the students and workers get their meals but he did not come back with his bowl to eat. He came much later and his bowl was empty."

"How does the old man explain this?"

"He says that he ate in a friend's room and came back when he was finished."

"I don't think the old man could have done it."

"How do you know this?" Mrs. Hua said. "I believe . . ."

Not for the first time Janet felt the acute frustration of not knowing the language, of having to speak at the mercy of another person. "Please. Tell him the old man eats dinner at exactly five-thirty every day. Nothing would make him go without his dinner."

She remembered how he watched the hand of the clock click another minute closer to the best time. She could almost feel with him the anticipatory juices in his mouth. He wet his lips with a very moist tongue. It was five-thirty. He had dropped from his distracted fingers those precious postage stamps he sold to the foreigners. Although he never let anyone touch them, he now made no move to stop her from riffling through them to select the most attractive ones. All he could think of was eating.

The stolid look on the face of the officer didn't change but she could tell he wasn't rejecting her ideas. He glanced at her several times while Mrs. Hua was translating, nodding his head infinitesimally.

"Anyhow," she went on, "he would never have had the strength." His hands trembled and he shuffled so slowly it was almost impossible to get to the telephone before the caller hung up, no matter how one sprinted to get to it as soon as one heard his knock on the door.

The officer made no comment except to motion with his hand that the interrogation was over.

6

As they walked across the compound to the classroom building, Janet asked Sally, "Where were you yesterday?"

"In town. Why?"

Her insouciance made Janet angry. "Why? Don't you know the whole staff was out looking for you? Everyone was very worried!" Here she was, casually heading for class, with no thought for the hysteria she had caused. Not only were they concerned about her safety, but the fact that she was a foreigner magnified their responsibility for her.

"I just felt rotten, so I decided to bike to town. Get some air."

"All night?"

She shrugged. "I met a friend at the hotel and decided to stay over. I got back about six this morning. What's all the fuss about?"

"You might have let someone know!"

"I left a note under Mrs. Hua's door. Didn't she tell you?"

There had been no note. Where *had* she been all night? That, Janet reminded herself, was no longer her concern; it was just nosiness.

Her students had already heard about what had happened to Mrs. Li. How had the news traveled so quickly to the dormitories on the other side of the compound? They were all talking at once when she came in. The class monitor spotted her and shushed them all to silence. For once they didn't smile and crowd around, eager to help her put her books and papers down, to practice a new English sentence, to ask for the meaning of an English word. They all sat and looked at her. The monitor rose and began to speak with some ceremony.

In China the monitor is a person with clout. He acts as liaison between students and teacher, seeing to it that both the students' and the teacher's rights are safeguarded. He will maintain order in the classroom if that is necessary and find materials for the teacher in the face of administrative stonewalling. The students take his position very seriously.

Now he spoke in his careful English. "Professor Aldane, please excuse, my English is not so good."

She made the customary vague demurral, and he cleared his throat and went on.

"Comrade Li is died. This is very bad trouble. Our unit is disgrace."

All community life was encompassed by the work unit. Students, faculty, restaurant workers, cleaners, were all part of the unit, which was administered by unit leaders called cadres. It was like living in a small town, where each person's behavior impacted forcefully on everyone else's life.

"Why?" she asked. "Do you think someone in the college killed her?"

"We do not know this. One person has done a terrible thing. Everyone will be . . . uh . . . the security police will . . . one person . . ." His English failed him.

"You mean until the murderer is found everyone will be suspected?"

"Yes. Suspected." He nodded in relief. "It is shame to us."

The others could be still no longer. Apparently they had been discussing the problem and arrived at the solution. "Professor, you must find the one who kill Mrs. Li."

"You have much knowledge of people."

"You understand what people do. You know why people . . ."

"You will know how to speak . . . how to ask questions."

She laughed. "Yeah, I'm great at asking questions—but not so great at answering them." She was very good at what she did, but she was constantly surprised that others expected from her wise pronouncements and instant solutions to complex problems.

"Yes, yes, you know much about many things. You will find who did this."

"I appreciate your confidence in me, but I don't think the police will want me to interfere. In my country they feel they are the experts in solving crimes and they are the ones to ask the questions."

"They will be honored," the monitor assured her. "The soldiers are not wise. They are uneducated peasants."

"Yes, they will ask questions—and ask and ask, for a very long time. They will stop our work. We will not be able to study. This must not happen!"

"We will tell the Principal. You are the one to help. You understand the importance of our studies."

"The Principal has the power to tell the army?"

"He will do it when we tell him," the monitor answered resolutely.

Pressure from students was not viewed lightly by college administrators and faculty. It was students who had routed the faculty during the Cultural Revolution and forced many of them into the countryside. Some high-level faculty dressed like workers and shaved only sporadically, fearful of being identified as the intellectuals they were. And although administrators—like administrators everywhere—enjoyed the perks of their positions, they rode in chauffeured cars with one wary eye on the mood of the students. If letting the foreign professor ask questions kept things quiet, they would be satisfied.

She had an idea that this murder would not be solved through clues left at the scene of the crime. Observing the people involved and assessing their characters was exactly what she was good at. And the officer in charge had seemed interested in her opinion. Maybe she could be useful.

She remembered the conventions and expressed her sympathy for the death of Mrs. Li. Although no one in the college seemed to like the woman, she was, after all, one of their own, a leader in their society. And Janet really did sympathize. "I'm sorry this happened. She didn't deserve to die that way."

"Mrs. Li is honored cadre. She is soldier with Chairman Mao." That was still important. The excesses of the Cultural Revolution had not erased the memory of awe and respect elicited by the mention of the Chairman's name.

"She is very strong for the revolution. She does not . . . uh . . . permit to destroy it."

"She loves China."

No expression of grief at her death. Only a sort of collective discomfort that someone of prominence had been killed in their midst.

7

Janet was drawn again to the scene of the murder. She turned onto the path and picked her way across the sand and dirt, stepped over scattered bricks and walked through the entrance of the unfinished building. No one was around to question or stop her. She was curious to know exactly what could be seen from a window on one of the upper floors. She ignored the sensible question that came to her: Who would be watching from an empty building?

The air inside was damp and she felt as if she were in an echoing concrete box. It got darker as she went higher, until she was feeling her way along the rough cold wall. On the first landing she groped through a half-open door into light again. It was a single room with a sashless window that looked out at the Foreign Students Building. The blue curtains across the way fluttered against the screens. It was very quiet. Directly below were the construction materials and the hill of sand where Mrs. Li had been found. She had no trouble seeing the small area clearly, but how much could be seen at night? Unless there were lights in the windows on the lower floor of the Foreign Students Building, it would be pitch dark below.

She stopped at the head of the stairs to look up toward the next floor. No point climbing up; the next floor would yield no more information than this one.

Suddenly, out of the dark, someone rushed past her, slamming her against the rough concrete. She scrabbled frantically for a hand-hold, found nothing, and stumbled down several steps, landing hard sitting down. Her breath came out in an explosion as if she had held it coming down, and her heart thumped erratically. She jumped up and—in the dark—bolted down the remaining stairs and out of the door. With not a glance behind her, she ran around the building and back to her room and fell into a chair.

When she could think again she decided it had been a good idea and that she would have to go back to look around on the other floors. Maybe she could find something that would lead her to an eyewitness of the crime. There was nothing to be afraid of, she told herself firmly. Obviously the person who had knocked her down did not want to harm her; he—or she—was just trying to get out without being recognized.

Inside the Foreign Students Building, behind the glass-partitioned cubicle that served as a front desk, another soldier was questioning the old man and Chang. A bed almost filled the small space, and now they sat side by side on the grimy pallet that each took turns sleeping on. They didn't look frightened. The old man was doing most of the answering. Good heavens! she thought. Have they been answering questions for four hours?

One of the three soldiers listening at the entrance to the cubicle saw her and came up. She smiled and shrugged her shoulders when he said something to her in Chinese. *"Bu dong."* She had learned very quickly how to say "I don't understand." A look of annoyance crossed his face and she grinned at him. I know just how you feel, she thought. Why the hell doesn't everybody speak Chinese?

He turned away abruptly and went to interrupt the man who was asking questions. They held a quick conference, the one who had talked to her jerking his head in her direction. She ambled down the corridor to her room. If they wanted her, they knew where to find her. Closing the door behind her, she breathed a deep sigh. Always so lovely to be home—even if home right now was ten thousand miles from Philadelphia. If only she had her own bathroom, she could be happy here. If only she had a real toilet!

Colette, showing her around her new living quarters, had opened the door of the single stall in the bathroom and Janet had gawped. Whatever Colette had thought was causing that response, she had said, "Ah yes. The Chinese, zey are veree sporting." Sporting?

How could she ever have imagined that there wouldn't be a toilet like the ones she was accustomed to, but only one recessed into the floor? Talk about culture shock! For a week she had been in culture coma! For a while she had been afraid that the lack of a toilet bowl would be her pivotal experience in China. But she was learning to manage. These days she peed on her shoes only two times out of three.

She sat in one of the two plastic easy chairs for a moment. A knock brought her to her feet again. She had got into the habit of locking her door because maids and other workers didn't bother to knock. Chinese friends knocked and then immediately turned the knob without waiting for an invitation to enter. Then it took minutes to urge them over the threshold, while they stood politely smiling and bowing. It might be fun to try living with her door unlocked—it lent a sort of openness and candor to human relationships—if you didn't mind being surprised in your underwear regularly.

This time it was Sally at the door. "PLA everywhere," she announced.

"Come on in. Do they have any idea yet who did it?"

"They don't seem to. They're questioning everyone."

My gosh, she's tall, Janet thought. She must be almost six feet! Mrs. Li was even shorter than me—certainly not more than four foot eleven. She could knock us both over with one swipe. Aloud she said, "Well, I suppose everyone in the building ought to be questioned. People were getting pretty fed up with the situation. Or not fed enough." She grimaced. "Maybe somebody finally exploded and . . ."

"I wasn't even here last night. *I* have nothing to tell!"

"Oh, I'm not serious. No one kills a person for turning off the hot water or buying rotten food."

Occasionally, Janet had the feeling that Sally needed buffering from some of the harsher realities. Now she fought it—she didn't want to feel that way after Sally's disappearance. Mrs. Hua would probably excuse her: "Oh, she is very young." Janet's response would be: "Oh, she is very irresponsible." Somehow, Sally's approach to teaching reflected on the importance of her own job.

Sally was saying something.

"What? I'm sorry, I didn't hear."

"The undergraduate students hated her. Mrs. Li. Any one of them could have killed her."

"The Chinese students? Why would they hate her? They had nothing to do with her."

"Oh, some of them did. It could have been one of them," she insisted.

Janet waited for some amplification, but Sally said nothing more. She just stood there looking at Janet as if it were now up to her to understand. Janet let it go. She hadn't much faith in Sally's powers of observation or reasoning, and she was apparently done with communicating for the time being. Nor had she said much at the interrogation before the officer had let them go. But there was something going on with her—something she was hiding.

8

Lunch was ready. She could not imagine what kind of catastrophe would interfere with the preparation of a meal. Although they spent no time lingering over coffee at the table like Westerners, the Chinese people ate with gusto and appreciation. That was why her complaints about the sheer awfulness of the food in this dining room had elicited such shocked commiseration.

The dining room staff did not eat the same things they served the foreign students and Janet and Sally. Even Colette did not eat well, although she paid twice what the others paid and had her four-course meals brought to her at the table. She was even given a paper napkin when she asked for it. There were no napkins for the others who paid for only one course. No one had given Colette a choice when she came to live in the building. Janet had insisted on only one course when she learned that the African students had this arrangement. There didn't seem to be much point in paying more money only to get more of the dreadful food. She had the feeling that insisting on one course was somehow infra dig, especially for a professor. The communist Chinese were very class-conscious.

Janet brought her dish to the table where four of the eight resident African students sat. Petiri told her, "The old Comrade Li—someone has strangled her and also has put a knife in her ribs."

"Yes, I know. Have they questioned you?"

"No, not yet. They question the Chinese."

Ka Ka Chi broke in, laughing, "When they have enough stories about us, they will question us."

Colette, at the next table, heard him. "Yes, they will tell all the stories," she said. "I am sure they cannot wait to tell the police about these immoral foreigners. And how far is it from immorality to murder, not so?"

Her pretty face was very pale. She still had not combed the night-time tangle out of her short black curly hair. "Janet, you have had experience with this kind of thing, have you not? I do not trust the

PLA to find out the person who did this. Perhaps you can do something?"

"Colette, I can't even speak the language!"

"They will respect you because you are a professor. They will listen to you. I will interpret for you. If you do not, heaven knows how long it will go on—the questioning, the presence of soldiers! I will be prevented from working!"

"Are you afraid they will think you killed her?" Petiri asked conversationally.

"Do you know what she did to me?" she demanded as if to justify murder. "You would not believe it! She sent Mrs. Hua to tell me that I must have no men in my room! *Quel culot!* Me—a grown woman! She dares to listen at my door, to question the maids!"

"She hated foreigners! She'd do anything to make trouble for us —get us sent back home."

All heads turned toward Sally. No one had ever heard so vehement an opinion from her. And that was all the encouragement Colette needed. "I have opened my door quickly and one of the women has been looking through the keyhole! Zut! What a country! She did the same to Laura Qian. They make her life miserable."

Janet had heard it all from Laura herself. Laura Qian was Mrs. Hua's cousin. Like Janet, she had come from the United States the year before to teach English at the college, but the attitude of the Chinese toward her was quite different from what it was toward other Americans.

"That old doorman questions her every time she goes out. He wants to know where she's going and whom she's going to see. He thinks because she's Chinese he can do this to her," Janet said.

"It is that Mrs. Li who encourages this. She makes . . . made life impossible!"

"That reminds me—have you seen Laura? Seems to me I haven't seen her since yesterday at breakfast." It was odd that no one at the college appeared to be concerned about her.

"She did not come home last night?"

"I don't think so. I heard something across the hall, but not from Laura's room."

"Hah! She is happy to be away from here and from that old witch!" Colette said. Then she remembered. "She does not know about Mrs. Li!"

"She may have trouble if her cousin finds out that she's gone."

"Ah yes, the helpful Mrs. Hua sides with the old Li."

"Not always, Colette. Didn't she intercede for you?" According to Mrs. Hua's own account, she had told Mrs. Li and the other cadres, "What does it matter what a foreign woman does with other foreigners? Say nothing. She will leave in a few months." At any rate, Colette had not been asked to leave, as might have happened. But instead of letting the matter drop, Colette had confronted Mrs. Li and there had been a noisy row. She detested the old woman and never stopped telling everyone so. Able to express her complaints in Chinese, she spoke volubly and at length to the workers in the building. But they were all Mrs. Li's friends and Janet could hear the protest in their answers even though she didn't understand the words.

"Oh, I am certain Laura is all right." Colette had already lost interest in somebody else's problem. Concern about her own was first. "Say you will discover the one who murdered Li!"

"Sure I will," she said soothingly. Her sincere sympathy for the frightened young woman obscured the skepticism. Colette was satisfied.

Janet wasn't as certain as everyone else seemed to be that she could solve the murder, but her curiosity was enough to get her involved even if no one had asked for her help. Just wanting to learn more about how the People's Liberation Army went about solving crimes would have been magnet enough. Her four years as social scientist with the Philadelphia police department had exposed her firsthand to American law enforcement procedures and caught her up in the fascination of understanding criminals—especially those who were not habitual criminals. She was impulsive too: whatever she thought was quickly followed by action. It was not possible for her to stay out of things.

9

The swinging door to the dining room opened and Masomakali, the student from Nigeria, shambled in. He was dressed outlandishly in bright yellow bell-bottom pants and a pink dress shirt, an apple hat tilted over one eye. And he wore a tie, that anti-revolutionary symbol of capitalism. He put one on periodically to express his contempt for the Chinese who rejected him, ostracized him, prevented him from making friends with other young men and women his age.

"Where have you been?" Janet smiled, greeting him in the Chinese way.

"I have been saving my life," he answered. He sat at the table smiling into space until Ka Ka Chi reminded him, "Your food is ready."

He eased himself to his feet and wandered over to the counter, where his plate had been resting for some time, carried it carefully back, sat down, and didn't touch it.

"Eat," Ka Ka Chi said to him.

He nodded, picked up the fork and put it down again. He's doped up to the eyeballs, Janet thought, and wondered what he was capable of in this condition. He seemed amiable enough, but when he caught her looking at him speculatively, he responded with a quick and great irritability. "The professor, she does not approve of me. What is ze matter, madame, am I not pleasing to you?"

She shrugged but he wouldn't let it alone, standing up to his full six foot four and declaiming for the whole dining room: "I save my life, but ze professor, she does not approve. She also does not understand. It is my life, do you hear? My life!"

She took up her chopsticks. Suddenly, they flew from her hand. Her fingers stung with the blow. How fast he was! She hadn't even seen him move toward her! Ka Ka Chi jumped up and grabbed him and suddenly he was smiling again. *"Mon ami,"* he cooed. *"Cher ami."* And he got the other man into a strangling bear hug. Ka Ka Chi moved them both around the table and got him into the chair again.

They all toyed with their food a while. She had a mental picture of Masomakali looming over Mrs. Li. Had he, under the influence of drugs, lost his temper with the super-moralist Mrs. Li? She might have threatened to cut off his drugs or have him arrested; he might have locked his massive hands around her throat and then gone amiably to bed. She felt a shiver up her spine.

"She wasn't young, but she was a vigorous person. She wouldn't easily be overpowered," she mused.

"*Comment?*"

"Oh, nothing, just thinking aloud. There had been no struggle where she was lying."

"Someone she knew well, perhaps, who struck her without warning," Ka Ka Chi suggested.

"Someone who hated her very much, to stab her *and* strangle her." She put her hand to her eyes to close out the fear and hatred and tried to think clearly. Masomakali might have strangled her in a sudden rage but would he have prepared himself with a knife and stabbed her? After so many years spent in preparing for his profession, would he kill rather than risk being sent home in disgrace?

He was sitting quietly now, looking intently at his untouched food, the anger that boiled in him momentarily capped.

"Chang told me she left here yesterday about five o'clock and she did not come to her house," Ka Ka Chi was saying.

"She went out back. Why would she do that?"

No one answered. They all sat silently picking at the food. Colette had also been served by one of the dining-room workers and her four small plates sat congealing. Now the cook himself came up to her and spoke. His manner was hostile and his speech explosive. Colette muttered in response without looking up and he left.

"What did he say?" Janet asked.

"He says nothing! Nothing!" She grabbed one of her plates and almost ran to an empty table, where she sat with her head in her hands.

That was a mistake, because Masomakali followed her. She usually managed to avoid being left alone with him because he kept insulting her. At least when others were around they were able to shut him up.

She had told Janet one evening why Masomakali was so antagonistic. "When I want to know if I like a man, I must go to bed with him. You understand?"

Janet gulped and nodded. "Completely."

"When I came here," she went on, "more than one year since, Masomakali was very nice. And he is tall and not ugly. One night, he stayed with me. In my bed. You understand?"

"Uh-huh."

"But I find I do not like him. I do not want him in my bed again. He is very angry."

"Yes, I can understand *that.*"

"Now when he sees me, he says terrible things to me, once even that I am whore!"

"That's not very sporting of him, is it?"

"Comment? I cannot sleep with him when I do not like him, *n'est-ce pas?*"

"No, you can't," she said, from the heart.

"Once he comes to my door at night and whispers to let him in. I did not. And he makes great noise hitting the door and shouting. It was terrible! I never speak of this, but he says terrible things always."

Now Janet felt sorry for her, alone at the table with him. The man was unstable. She should never have started anything with him. Colette had no judgment at all.

She sat there, shaking her head in what looked like pain while Masomakali kept talking. Janet winked to Sally and joined them. When she started to make conversation, Masomakali abandoned his lunch and left the room.

"I've just had something of a shock myself," Janet said. "I may have to solve this murder before they pin it on me."

"What do you mean? What has happened?" She had finally caught Colette's attention.

"They think I'm corrupting their youth. I may end up drinking hemlock for my sins."

"I do not understand."

"There's been some talk about my bad influence on the students." She shook her head, talking more to herself than to the French girl, who stared at her in bewilderment. "Some of those kids are very dissatisfied with what's happening in the country. The old ones know it and some of them would love to blame it on the influence of a decadent foreigner."

"Oh, I am so frightened! What will happen to us—to me?!"

"What is it? Why are you so afraid?"

"I will tell you, but you must swear to me you will say nothing to anyone."

"Of course. I swear."

"I was not in my room last night."

Janet looked at her, expecting more.

"They will discover that if they question me."

"Why does it matter? You're old enough to come and go as you please."

"Oh, you are naïve! I was with a Chinese student in his room. If the police discover this he will be in great trouble and I will be forced to leave China."

"You think they would really make you leave?"

"Oh yes. That Mrs. Li was the worst. But there are many others like her. They are—how do you say?—prudish, the Chinese. One can go to prison for this sort of thing."

"Prison! For spending the night with another adult?"

"Not the foreigners. But the Chinese, yes! He will be destroyed if they discover this."

"Sh . . . sh. Colette, who will tell them? He won't. And surely you won't."

"We have been seen together." She sat twisting her fingers, her eyes wide.

"How did you manage it anyhow? He can't possibly have a room of his own."

No one lived alone in China. Students were packed six in a room the size of her apartment kitchen at home. Teachers were married or had roommates. Couples waited for years to marry until they were assigned a room. An apartment was a rare luxury.

But Colette was not going to answer the question. Were people really spying on her or was she just suffering from the foreigners' paranoia that was endemic in China.

Janet gave up on it for now. "Come out back with me," she said. "I'd like to take another look at the unfinished building." She felt Colette resisting the pressure of her arm. "I think there was someone in there who may have seen the murder."

She gave a small scream and Janet saw her face go chalk white. "No, you must not go! You must say nothing. They know. The old man knows."

"Say nothing about what?"

"He will tell them that I left after lunch and did not return. And now you know."

"What do I know?"

"I came at three o'clock in the morning. I was forced to knock on the door so they would let me in."

So that was what had wakened her. "Oh hell. Whatever made you come in at that hour? If you stayed out all night you could just make it for breakfast or lunch and no one would be the wiser."

"I—what do you call it?—I felt panic. I thought they would search and find us. I ran."

"Find you where?"

"Oh, what does it matter? We are lost!"

The melodrama irritated her but Janet could appreciate Colette's fear. There was one thing Colette was constitutionally unable to do and that was to keep a secret—her own or anyone else's. Sooner or later Janet and the police would hear everything that Colette was keeping back. In a way, she loved the excitement of being in the spotlight, even though she was genuinely frightened. Maybe that was why she had run from the interrogation, because she knew the great temptation to tell it all.

"I saw him—the cook—near the hill of sand in the back."

"When? When did you see him?"

"Last night. At dinnertime. He was there."

Janet was skeptical. "What were you doing there?"

"No, no, you do not understand. I was not *there*. I saw him from above."

"Above? You can't see the place from upstairs in this building. Not unless you lean all the way out. You would have to take the screen out of the window."

"I saw him from the other building."

"The empty one? What were you doing in an empty building?"

"It is not—what did you say?—empty. Someone lives there. On the third floor."

"Who? Who lives there? There couldn't be any heat or electricity."

"There is no heat. But electricity, yes. One of the students who has graduated, he lives there."

"You were in his room?"

"He is my friend," she said, a little defensively.

"Your friend," Janet repeated noncommittally. What she was thinking was that Colette pursued friendship from bed to bed. It must have been the friend who almost caused her to break her neck. "I'd like to speak to your friend."

"No, no, it is not possible. If they are discovered they will be punished."

"They? How many people are living there?"

She shrugged. "Five, six. I am not certain."

"Okay, never mind. I'll find out what I have to. I'm going into the building now."

"You will be seen and the police will be told."

Janet considered. "You're right. I'll wait till it's dark." She sounded more sure of herself than she felt. She did not look forward to going into that shell at night.

"When it is night I will go with you. I will tell them that you try to help me—that you will tell no one."

Janet nodded but she doubted there would be anyone to talk to. Whoever had dashed past her would let the others know that their secret was out. "I must talk to them. One of them may have seen something else."

"I saw all. When I looked from the window the cook was sick."

"Sick?"

"Yes, you know. *Vomissement.* Sick."

"Oh," she said weakly. And thought: As if he'd just seen a dead body lying in the dirt? Had he stumbled on the body without informing the authorities? Was he afraid of the consequences of calling attention to himself in a society where keeping a low profile was the safe and sensible thing to do? Was it because he had disliked Mrs. Li so much that he had offered this final insult to her lifeless remains, letting her lie there undiscovered? Or . . . was he the one who had killed her?

"Did you see Mrs. Li lying there?"

"From the window I could see the hill, and the cook coming from behind it. But not her. I was afraid he had seen the light and would come up to see who was there. No one knows there is someone living in the building and that cook wishes to know everything so he will have power over people. He has great influence and the others fear him."

"Do you think he saw you?"

"Now I do not think so. He went away. I did not see him again that night. But the old man knows when I returned! He will tell the PLA!" And she was off again, shaking and crying and twisting her fingers.

"Sh . . . sh. It will be all right, Colette. You'll see. Just answer their questions, but don't say where you were."

"You must discover who did this, so there will be no trouble for me."

No trouble for her, perhaps, but there might be for her friends. Had one of the squatters seen Mrs. Li murdered? Had one of them murdered her?

10

After lunch everyone in China had his *wushui*, a two-hour nap to fortify himself for the afternoon's work. During *wushui* Janet usually read but she could feel the beginnings of an urge to get into bed after lunch. Now she sat comfortably slouched in an easy chair, her eyelids heavy, counting to herself the number of people who might have had reason to kill Mrs. Li. She thought of Wang Qu Qing again, the youngster with whom she had struck up a friendship. Even he might have had feelings strong enough for murder. Could he have blamed Mrs. Li for the constant reprimands he got from the college authorities for making friends with foreigners? He wanted desperately to go to an American university to study literature. Alone, with little encouragement, he had learned English, French, and "a little Russian." Although undergraduates were not invited to her lectures, he came to every one of them, asking probing questions, comparing her answers with information he got from his meager store of books. She was afraid he would never be permitted to study abroad. He was too outspoken, too mercurial in his loyalties, and he spent more time with foreign friends than he did with the other Chinese students.

Wang Qu Qing had told her about the catch-22 in the English-language examination, given by the Educational Testing Service of Princeton by arrangement with the Chinese government. Most American universities required a passing grade for admission, a grade that certified competence in English. Wang Qu Qing might scrape together the twenty-three-dollar fee to take the test, but it had to be paid in American dollars. Since it was illegal for Chinese people to be in possession of American money, it was clear that the government could control who would take the test.

She wanted very much to help him. She had discussed the matter with someone at the American embassy, trying to find a way to get around the fee requirement. Had information about her inquiry got back to the Chinese authorities? Had it become part of a dossier on her that could get her kicked out of China?

At exactly two-thirty, there was a knock at her door.

"Yue Zhen and Mr. Guo! How nice to see you both! Come in."

"Thank you, Professor. Thank you."

They stood just inside the door. He was a tall young man, his thick black hair meticulously combed, not a wrinkle in his white shirt. Up until the beginning of this year he had been a French teacher at the college. Since the number of students of French had dropped off, he had been told one morning that he was now an English translator. Did bureaucratic decisions ever reach this depth of idiocy in the United States?

She remembered the moment outside the barrier at the Beijing Airport when she felt her arm taken. "We warmly welcome you to our country." It sounded delightful. She had stepped off the plane after twenty-four hours and she still felt high.

"Thank you," she said. "I'm happy to be here." Her heart beat fast and her eyes sparkled.

The young man had had no trouble recognizing her, although he had responded with some skepticism to the description that his colleague in the United States had written. The *Meiguo ren*'s hair did indeed shimmer like silver in the incandescent light of the lounge as she turned from one to another of the welcoming committee and her bright green eyes almost transfixed the person she was looking at. Not a beautiful woman—especially to Asian eyes—but easily recognizable.

In the car, the woman in the front seat turned around. No smile. The driver kept his eyes on the road. No one said anything more for a while. "I hope you will like your *maison*," the young man said. "It is for foreigners only. Once a foreign teacher, the next year, she Chinese abroad. Therefore." He smiled.

She stared at him in bewilderment. "What?"

Later, Mrs. Hua told her that this young man was to be her guide and interpreter. Mr. Therefore dutifully arranged for sightseeing trips and followed her around, and she learned to smile and nod while he talked unintelligibly and she thought of other things.

Yue Zhen said in her breathy, hesitant English, "We are so sorry to disturb you."

"You're not disturbing me."

"You know about the old Li?" asked her husband.

"Yes." Was it possible that anyone did *not* know? "I'm so sorry about your mother, Yue Zhen."

"I have just learned it," Mr. Guo said. "I have been away from my house since a week." He had apparently rehearsed the sentence.

"Really?" He had missed several days of classes but it didn't seem that long since she had seen him around here. Perhaps she was mistaken.

"I visit my family in countryside. My father is ail."

"Oh," she said blankly. "Oh!" as understanding came. "Your father is ill! I'm sorry."

Another knock on the door, and the officer in charge came in. He said something to Mr. Guo.

"He wishes to ask me. I will go." As he started out the officer stopped him. "He asks *ici.* I will translate."

Oh, great! She felt one of her headaches coming on.

There was an exchange between them and the officer waited for Mr. Guo to tell her what was being said. "He asks if I am here. I say I am to my family, in Shanxi Province."

"Weren't you here yesterday, Mr. Guo? Before dinner? I don't think you were, Yue Zhen."

"My wife does not speak English well."

Yue Zhen's English was better than his, but she said nothing. How to tell if he was evading her question or if he was just not understanding what she had said? Maybe she hadn't seen him. At any rate, he offered no translation for the officer, and his wife just sat there.

The officer said something to him and she caught the words *wu dian ban*— five-thirty. She had not seen the old doorman until about six-thirty, when she had bought some postage stamps from him before the students had begun to gather. Chang had been sitting on the unmade bed scooping rice into his mouth from his dinner bowl. Who else had she seen? Had Mrs. Hua been there?

Not Guo's wife, she was sure now. Yue Zhen, intensely quiet for long minutes while the conversation in English went on around her, then producing a perfect English sentence—completely non sequitur—waiting for an answer from Janet, and retiring again into her head to formulate another sentence. Each word was enunciated carefully, with long, breathy aspirations between words, the final stop accompanied by a small, satisfied smile. Janet didn't think she ever really heard the answer; she was content merely to get one. She found herself as usual fighting the small nudge of dislike she felt for the young woman.

And Mr. Xu was there, unshaven, in his grimy undershirt with its almost artistically arranged holes. With, as always, the placating smile.

Mr. Guo was speaking. "He asks do I like Mrs. Li. I like him. *Tout le monde* like him. He is honored revolutionary."

She said nothing. He would translate only what he could understand or what he wanted the officer to hear. The officer seemed to have run out of questions but he made no move to leave, so Janet motioned him to a chair and asked her own questions.

"Your father must be feeling very bad, Yue Zhen. Have you seen him?"

"My father?" She looked puzzled.

"Yes, your father. He must be feeling very bad about what happened to your mother."

"My father is dead."

For a moment, Janet felt dizzy. Not another m——!

"He died in the Long March."

Blank.

"He was a brave man."

"Your mother's husband is not your father?"

"My mother is married five years. He is a younger man. Younger to my mother. A professor at university."

"I thought your mother did not like professors."

She gave a small laugh and took a breath. "She does not like professors but she wants this one."

Janet grinned, then sobered quickly. "Is he very unhappy now?"

"He is unhappy, yes."

Murder in China

Janet took the plunge. One could not be fastidious if one was going to play detective. "Did they have a good marriage?"

She shrugged. "He is very quiet man, says little. My mother says much."

"Was he happy with your mother?"

"I do not think so. My mother tells him what to do. She takes book from him. Says he must work in countryside, to learn from peasants. He says he is teacher, not peasant. She is very angry."

That must have been a happy marriage! She glanced at the officer, wondering what he would think of all this. "Do you like him, Yue Zhen?"

"My mother tells me he is weak. For a long time he stays in his room at university when others go to fields. They put *das bao* to him. Denounce him. Very disgrace."

Janet remembered the stories told her by some of the undergraduates, how posters had been put up on the walls of houses denouncing the people inside, how some of them had been forced to stand in the street wearing signs hung on their necks detailing their crimes against the revolution. Tong Ching Mei had seen her father with such signs hanging from his neck, disgraced, ruined, his job with the government lost. All because a picture of Chairman Mao had fallen unnoticed from the wall and been found under his bed. Her mother, ashamed and frightened, had cut her wrists. Had Mrs. Li symbolized for this student what the world had done to her family?

"I've never seen Mrs. Li's husband here. When she didn't come home last night, did he notify the police?"

"I do not think so," Mr. Guo began.

"Ask the officer, Mr. Guo. I'd like to know."

"Husband is here now. I will bring." He darted from the room. The officer looked nonplussed, then followed him out.

Yue Zhen sat on the stool in the corner with her knees together and her feet apart, like a little girl. Her hands, fisted, rested on her knees. "I feel very bad," she said. "I do not know what to do."

It was hard to remember that she was a twenty-eight-year-old woman, she sounded so childlike. Her hair, cut short like her mother's, fell over her face as she bent her head.

"Who could have done such a thing?" The question could be taken for an expression of sympathy or as a request for information. Yue Zhen was probably the one most likely to throw light on her mother's relationships, most likely to know of some motive for wanting her mother dead.

She looked up, her eyes intent on Janet's face. "My mother," she said, "was not loved."

Janet gasped. Yue Zhen went on as if she had not heard. "Many people come to her. For back door. She says no. They were very angry to her. Many people."

Back door. The bland little phrase that covered a morass of favoritism, black-market trading, corruption of all kinds. If you wanted to keep your son in Beijing instead of seeing him transferred to some distant province where engineers or teachers were needed, knowing someone of influence could get his transfer canceled. A larger apartment that became available might be yours if you had back-door access through a friend in authority.

But Mrs. Li would be no one's back door. Janet remembered . . . Yue Zhen had come to her the week after her arrival in China. "I want to be your friend," she had said. "I want you to be my teacher." And then, almost in the same breath, had come the real reason for the overture. "When you go to the Friendship Store I will go with you."

"Uh, of course. If you like. Is there something you want to buy?"

The Chinese were not permitted to shop at the Friendship Store, but it was not unusual for foreigners to escort a Chinese person into the store, telling the guards at the door that he was acting as interpreter and guide. Once inside, the Chinese gave money to the foreigner to make a purchase. It was a sad transaction all around, and she felt outraged on behalf of the ordinary Chinese person who was not permitted to enter where foreigners could go freely. The old foreign concessions in Shanghai had done the same—and the revolution had destroyed them, but it had never destroyed the xenophobia they had reinforced.

"I want to buy a fine bicycle," Yue Zhen had told her.

"You have a bicycle, don't you? I've seen you on one."

"I want a *fine* one. It is not a fine one."

"Don't you need special permission to buy a bicycle?"

"I will give you the money."

"But if I buy the bicycle, then I'll have to sell it back to the store when I leave China. That's the law."

"They will do nothing to you. You are a professor."

"Why doesn't your mother help you? She's got a lot of influence."

"My mother will not do things back-door—I must wait for permission."

"I'm sorry, Yue Zhen. I'll be glad to get you into the store but I'm not signing my name and buying a bicycle. I don't want to get into trouble." She was annoyed that Yue Zhen expected this of her and more annoyed that she felt compelled to refuse. She thought it was wrong that foreigners could buy bicycles, when the Chinese needed them desperately for transportation and had to wait years sometimes before their turn came up to get one. She was torn between wanting to help someone she believed had a right to a new bike and fearing the repercussions of breaking the law. She had never really liked Yue Zhen after that. She didn't like herself either for refusing.

Now she felt sorry for her, she looked so unhappy. What had she said? Her mother was not loved. Did she include herself in this assessment? Was her mother "not loved" by her too?

"Do you think one of those people that your mother turned away might have done this?"

Yue Zhen just looked at her and said nothing. Janet had the feeling she had plenty to say.

11

In a few moments Mr. Guo was back with Mrs. Li's husband in tow. Janet felt vaguely embarrassed, as if she had been caught gossiping behind his back.

"Here is Jiao Zhong En," Mr. Guo introduced him.

"I am pleased to meet you," he said in perfect English.

"I just told Mr. Guo that I would like to meet you. I didn't mean for him to . . ."

"It is quite all right. I have been wanting to meet you too. Mr. Xu has told me much about you, about how you have helped him." Mr. Xu was the faculty member who came to her classes and her evening conversation group, always looking so bedraggled.

"I'm so sorry about your wife."

He was a very good-looking man. Tall for a Chinese, with thick black hair shot through with gray. He didn't look more than fifty-five or so—younger than Mrs. Li.

"Mr. Guo tells me you teach at Beijing University."

"Yes, I am a social scientist. We are working now to rebuild our department. It was destroyed during the Cultural Revolution, you know. The professors were sent to work in the countryside."

There was no trace of bitterness in the quiet voice. His small smile as he talked seemed to assume that she understood the foolishness of human beings and the sadness of events. "You are a psychologist?" he asked her.

"More a social psychologist."

"Ah, yes, you study group rather than individual behavior. You must find China very interesting—different than your studies in the United States."

"It's frustrating not to be able to speak Chinese. I sometimes feel such a fool, needing other people to speak for me."

"I assure you, Professor, you impress no one as a fool." He spoke seriously but he almost seemed to be teasing her.

"You speak English very well." She hoped she didn't sound patronizing. She really was impressed with his fluency and his slightly English accent.

"I spent some time in England. And, of course, I continue to study and to speak English when I can."

They were quiet for a while, the air heavy with unasked questions. Then he said, "I have heard that the students wish you to discover who did this . . . this . . ." He faltered, the deed too much even for his elemental calm.

She nodded. "They're very concerned. They want the criminal found."

"I think, perhaps, they are concerned to have the security police interrupting their studies."

"Oh no! They're very sorry about what's happened. They respected Mrs. Li."

He looked at her without saying anything, until she was compelled to look away. Yue Zhen got them back on track. "Jiao Zhong En visits Mr. Xu on night when my mother is . . . is . . ."

"That is true. I was at Xu's house. Then he left to go to your English group. I went er . . . uh . . . away."

"Oh, please." She was embarrassed.

"No." He waved her protest aside. "I want to tell you. The students wish you to help. I will tell you what you want to know."

Well, if he didn't mind . . . She wanted to find out more about this man whose manner made her think he didn't care one way or the other if the murderer was identified.

"Your wife did not come home yesterday evening?"

"No, but that was not unusual. Her work kept her busy. And she had meetings," he added vaguely.

"You weren't worried when she didn't come home all night?"

"I did not know she was not at home. It was quiet. I slept soundly."

She almost had a sense of the peace he felt in his home when his wife was not there.

"In the morning, I thought she had left early. She often did. Or, perhaps, that she had stayed at work. I felt a little uneasy, but I knew she had a room in this building where she could have stayed when she pleased."

She found him very attractive—his looks, his quiet manner, his intelligence—but, she thought, that was rather an obvious lie.

"You . . . er . . . didn't . . . uh . . . ?" How to ask him if he and his wife shared the same bed? It would sound not only indelicate, especially in China, but stupid. Not only must they have shared a bed, there would not have been room for more than one bed in their home.

He smiled, understanding her discomfort. "You are quite right in what you are thinking. In the usual situation a husband would know that his wife had not come home all night. But you see, we have two rooms. One is on the floor above the other. My wife is . . . was . . . a very important woman."

She wondered why she suddenly felt so pleased. "Have the police questioned you?"

"Yes. I could tell them nothing. It would not be unusual for my wife to walk to the back, even with the building materials all about. She often walked around here to see that everything was in order."

"Mrs. Li did everything she could to help China achieve the Four Modernizations, didn't she?"

"Yes, she was a true patriot. Unfortunately she saw no value in intellectual work. She believed it was the intellectuals who had almost destroyed the revolution, and would still do so if they were not watched and controlled." He glanced ruefully at Mr. Guo. He had begun to speak a little more quickly so Guo wouldn't understand.

"Then why . . . ?" she started to ask impulsively, then stopped in confusion.

"Why did she marry someone like me?" he finished the question for her. He was trying not to grin.

"It certainly does seem an odd choice for her," she said at last. "If she had no use for intellectuals, why would she marry one?"

He was suddenly serious again and a little pedantic. "It is difficult to explain. She embodied the Chinese ambivalence about learning. On the one hand, she mistrusted and had contempt for a class that had perpetuated feudalism; on the other hand, she had the traditional Chinese respect for learning. It was, in a peculiar way, a source of pride to her to be married to a professor."

There was an echo of loneliness in what he said, as if his wife's pride had been for a symbol rather than for the man. The loneliness touched the feeling in her. There were times since she had come to China when the excitement and curiosity were not enough, and she missed her family and friends. She had not been inside a real home since her arrival.

Mr. Guo stood up suddenly. "We must go now," he announced.

"Yes." Jiao Zhong En stood also. "We have taken too much of your time."

"Oh no. I'm happy you came. Please come again."

"I would like that." He bowed slightly.

In the Chinese custom she walked with her guests out of the building. In the American custom she shook hands with Jiao Zhong En. She thought the pressure of his fingers and the way he looked at her meant she would see him again soon.

As they stood in the courtyard finishing their conversation, Yanmin, one of the workers in the building, passed them. Mrs. Li's husband, son-in-law, and daughter all greeted her. She smiled shyly and hurried inside. Jiao Zhong En looked after her as they said their goodbyes.

Janet hoped to see him again soon. She also hoped he hadn't killed his wife.

12

The old man and Chang still sat on the bed being interrogated, although the questions and answers seemed more leisurely now, more chatty, as if no one knew exactly where to go from here. Wang Qu Qing came into the courtyard, his head up, smiling—looking for trouble. He must have known the police were everywhere. She'd keep him with her, act as his excuse for being there.

"Wang Qu Qing, would you like to be my interpreter?"

"Oh yes, I like that. For always?"

"No, just for now. I'd like to ask the *maipiaoyuan*—the sellers of food tickets—some questions. Will you come with me?"

How she wished she could engage the workers in casual conversation and get what they knew about the comings and goings the evening of the murder. If she appeared now with an interpreter and started asking direct questions they had a perfect right to tell her to buzz off. Or would the polite, talkative Chinese be willing to tell her what she wanted to know about their friends?

"Yes, I will come."

Everyone who ate in the college dining rooms—foreigners in this one and the Chinese students and faculty in their own—paid for their meals with meal tickets purchased in advance. In the office of the Foreign Students Building two women sat, one counting out the tickets, one taking the money. The office was just large enough for the two facing desks. As they did all day, the ticket sellers were knitting with dark blue wool, probably sweaters against the coming winter winds.

Their talking continued when Janet and Wang Qu Qing came in, only they had turned from each other to include the newcomers. When one stopped for breath, the other started. And then Wang Qu Qing became a third, the three of them going on and on, sometimes serious, sometimes laughing, occasionally glancing at Janet, who stood there smiling, looking from one to another.

Finally she broke in. "Wang Qu Qing, what are they saying?"

"They are sad for Mrs. Li. They are afraid."

"What are they afraid of?"

"Uh . . . uh . . . traitor . . . Yes, traitor to revolution kills cadre."

"Do they know who it is?"

He shook his head. "Maybe foreigners."

She brushed that off. "Did Mrs. Li talk to them about anyone she was afraid of? Anyone who threatened her?"

"Threatened?"

"Anyone who said he would kill her?"

They talked again for a long time—all at once.

"Wang Qu Qing!"

Silence. Then: "They say she fights only a little with the cook. But they are friends. Not kill."

Maybe he killed her only a little, Janet sighed in frustration. At home such an interview would be much more satisfactory. She was a friendly person, quick to see the flip side of things, reducing commonplace pomposities to absurdity. Speaking through an interpreter deprived her of more than just words; her whole personality was diminished.

"Ask them if they saw her husband here yesterday."

"He does not come here much. Maybe he is here yesterday."

She looked sharply at him. "Did they say that—or is that your idea?"

"They say he is not here. Only maybe."

She rolled her eyes in exasperation. "Will you ask them very clearly if they remember seeing him here yesterday. Tell them to answer *shi* or *bu shi*—yes or no."

He grinned at her Chinese and asked the question, exaggerating his enunciation. The women shook their heads and shrugged. Neither *shi* nor *bu shi*. She sighed. Would they tell her if he was here?

"Did they see her with anyone before she left?"

The door flew open and Chang stood there—and all four of them were talking at once. Janet waved feebly in their general direction and left. As Wang Qu Qing caught up with her she could hear the talk settle down to a continuous cadence of rising and falling tones punctuated by the click of knitting needles.

"Chang is afraid of Li. She tells him he will not work here."

"Oh? Why?"

"He talks too much to foreigners. He does not clean."

"Do they think he could have killed her?"

"They say he is . . ." He tapped his head. "Maybe he kills."

Was it really possible, or was he just a convenient scapegoat?

"Well, thanks for your help."

"Yes, I must go. Goodbye."

She laughed and waved him off.

13

The scratching on her door meant that Colette wanted company. Good! Maybe a couple of glasses of sherry would calm her down enough so they could explore the empty building as soon as dusk fell.

As she closed the door behind her, it slammed open again, almost knocking her down.

"Qu'est-ce-que tu as fait? Tu m'as détruit!"

"Quoi? Vous êtes fou!"

"What the hell's going on? What do you mean by bursting in here?"

Masomakali continued to shout at Colette in French and she kept denying whatever it was he was accusing her of. Several times she screamed, *"C'est le chef! C'est le chef! Pas moi!"* It's the cook, not me!

"Now both of you, calm down! BE QUIET!" Janet yelled. She wasn't a teacher for nothing.

After a breath, Colette said, "I told them nothing. Why should I tell them? I do not want them even to think about me. I want only to be left alone to do my work."

"Who, then? Who tells the police that I come to your door?"

"It was the chef . . . the cook. He said that to me too."

"So what if he came to your door? Why should that matter to the police?"

"He tells that Masomakali is drunk and he comes to my door and threatens to break it down. He tells that Masomakali, when he drinks, is violent."

"Oh yes, they think all Africans are—how you say?—animals. With drink, I do murder!"

"But isn't the cook afraid that you'll tell the police that he sells drugs?" Janet asked him.

"Comment?"

"I've seen you buying drugs from him. It's no secret around here."

"Je ne . . ."

"Tell him what I said, Colette." Colette translated that and then went on to translate the whole exchange into French.

"Oh no," Masomakali said. "The cook knows I will not tell. He sells life to me. If I tell, I am lost."

"But if you're arrested for murder you won't get any drugs in jail. You're not any better off by keeping it secret."

"Ah, that man, he has back door everywhere! In prison he will not abandon me." He put his head in his hands. "I wish I could kill *him,* " he moaned in despair.

"How do you know the cook told the police about Masomakali's coming to your door?" Janet asked Colette.

"I came home earlier. The soldiers and the cook were speaking in the old man's room. I heard everything. They did not know I was there."

"Then the soldier came to my room. He does not arrest me but I think it will be soon."

"Did you kill the woman, Masomakali?"

He looked at her for a long moment. "You think I killed her?" His voice was infinitely sad. "I have been here eight years. For eight years I feel like killing but I do not. One year more and I am in my own country. Here I live; I kill no one."

"Did you see her yesterday before she died?"

"I saw her. She talks to the fat one."

"Oh? Where did they talk?"

"They walk to the back where the new building is, but they do not see me."

"What did you hear? If the cook had something to do with her death, it would get us all off the hook."

Colette didn't understand the colloquialism but she got the point well enough, and translated the question.

"I must not say anything! The cook must not go away! I would not be able to live!"

"But if you're arrested for murder you could be executed. Is that what you want?"

"I will die! I cannot! I will die and that will be the end!"

"I promise you, Masomakali. I won't tell the police what you tell me. Just tell me what you heard so I will know what further questions to ask of the others."

She had no idea how she would keep this promise if it turned out that the information revealed the cook as the murderer. Ah well, she would deal with this if it became necessary.

"You will say nothing?"

"I promise."

"Tell her, Masomakali. She will help us all. She knows much about these things."

"Yes, I will tell you. You will not tell the police?" He wanted reassurance again. He would tell and then regret that he had. "The cook, he says it takes much time for him to buy the food. That is why he is not here. She says he is away too much, *n'est-ce pas?*"

"Is that all?"

"No, that is just the beginning. They get very angry together. Perhaps he kills her, but I do not believe it, no."

"What else did they argue about?"

"*Elle s'accuse.* She accuse him to take the money."

"What money?"

"The money he has to buy the food. For the meals in the dining room."

"I knew it! I knew he must be pocketing the money. We each pay about six *kwai* a day for meals. For six *kwai* we could eat like kings."

"She says the meals should be better or there will be trouble for them all."

"Hah! She admitted they were awful. She cared enough to say something."

"No, she does not care. She tells him that. She cares nothing for the foreigners. But she says you complain to the Principal of the college and she is shamed. She says the foreign professor comes to help China and she does not eat. If she is sick, it will be bad thing for the unit."

Nothing like a good offense, Janet thought. She pushes to get me kicked out for subversion before I can get her kicked out for rotten housekeeping. "What does he say to that?" she asked Masomakali.

"He says he does his best. He buys the best vegetables and meat. He buys fish too and that is very dear. But the foreigners complain about everything. She shouts at him that she will make another one the cook and he is very angry. He tells her he will denounce her and she will be disgraced."

"Denounce her for what?"

"I am not certain. He speaks very low and I cannot hear all. It is something of the girl, Yanmin. He says he knows why she is here. Mrs. Li becomes very quiet. She says nothing more of the cooking or the money."

"We must speak to the girl," said Colette. "We will demand that she tell us."

"Slow down! You can demand all you like, but what if she doesn't know anything? You'll just make people afraid to talk to us and we'll learn nothing more."

"Yes, yes. We will leave it to you. You are very wise."

She tried to look wise.

"What time was this, when you heard them arguing?"

"Before dinner. About five o'clock."

And at five-thirty Colette had seen him being sick. It certainly put him on the spot at the right time.

"Did you see them leave?"

"The cook left. I did not see the woman go. Then I went to my room."

Someone else could have gone out back right after the cook left and killed her. Then why would he go back again? To have a last word? And when he found her dead, he was sick. That could have been a shocker—just having a fight with someone and finding her dead a few minutes later. Aloud, she said, "It doesn't sound like he had reason to kill her. It was a standoff."

"Standoff?"

"Impasse."

"Ah yes, impasse. She accuse him, he accuse her. They have both to fear each other, so each says nothing of the other. Maybe now we will have another cook. That will not be such a bad thing."

Masomakali shrugged and said something. Janet looked to Colette questioningly. "He says the cook will remain. Those in power are his friends. Ask Guo. He is his good friend."

The immaculate Mr. Guo a friend of the cook? That was an odd combination.

14

She forgot about the sherry and ushered the two out, glad for a little quiet and solitude. But she was startled and dismayed to hear sobbing through the plaster wall that separated her room from Sally's. Sally seemed so impervious to events and to the people around her, as if she had a secret agenda through which she moved without considering anyone. Janet didn't think she could ever feel strongly enough to cry about anything. Now she regretted her own insensitivity; Sally *was* very young—and far from home.

Fatigue rolled over her at the prospect of soothing yet another distraught soul, but she pulled herself to her feet and went to ask Sally what was wrong. The answer she got added two more suspects to the list.

"They'll think I killed Mrs. Li," Sally sobbed. "It will all get back to my parents. They'll never let me do anything again."

"Sally, if the police are ever convinced that you killed Mrs. Li your parents will be the least of your troubles. Would you like to tell me what happened?"

"Everybody must have heard about it." And she burst into sobs again.

Janet patted her back and brought her a drink of tepid water from the carafe next to the hot-water jug. She sipped and made a face, but she stopped crying for a while.

"Everybody must have heard about what?" Janet prompted her.

"The fight I had with Mrs. Li."

"You fought with her too? I never heard you complain to her."

"I didn't! I didn't want any trouble. The Principal knows my parents. If they thought I wasn't happy here, they'd make me come home and go back to school."

So that's how she had got the job! Her parents probably still knew people in the country from their missionary days.

Janet asked another question quickly to forestall the tears that almost started again. "You had a fight before you went to town?"

"Ye-e-s," she wailed.

"Can you tell me? Maybe it's not as awful as you think."

"She was horrible. She yelled and yelled at me, and I couldn't understand what she was saying."

Janet patted her hand and urged her to sip the water again. The rest came out in an embarrassed and horrified whisper, broken by sobs and hiccups and quick sips of water. "She unlocked my door. She had her own key. She just . . . just . . . just w-walked in on us! Oh, my parents will kill me. It isn't as if we don't love each other. We do! We do! He'll be kicked out of college and sent back to his hometown. I'll never see him again. Oh, it was awful. I'm so scared."

"Who was it, Sally?" Janet asked softly. "Not Wang Qu Qing?"

"Who? Certainly not!" She was momentarily distracted from her grief and fear and gave the older woman an indignant glare. "You think I'm a cradle snatcher? He's just a kid!" Then she was off again, wailing and hiccuping. "It was someone else. You don't know him. Oh, what am I going to do?"

Janet sighed. An undergraduate. She'd gone to bed with an undergraduate. The college authorities would take a very hard line about such a thing. The boy could even be sent to the equivalent of reform school for "reeducation." What a mess!

"How did he get in without being stopped at the door?"

She pointed to her window. The screen had been removed and it would take very little agility to duck through when the coast was clear.

"The police know who the boy is?"

"No. They asked me but I wouldn't tell them. Everybody here heard the fight but Lu . . . uh . . . he got out the window when Mrs. Li came in."

"Did she get a look at his face?"

"I don't know."

"Maybe she died before she could tell anyone. When did it happen?"

"Yesterday. During *wushui*. She ran out and I thought she was trying to find him."

"Do you think she caught up with him?"

"I don't know. You don't think *he* could have . . . ?"

"I don't think he killed her then. She was still alive at five o'clock. Unless he came back later . . ."

"Oh my God." She sounded very tired—too tired to cry anymore. Love did not deserve such anguish.

What would happen if some of the foreign newsmen stationed in Beijing got hold of this? Murder and illicit sex in a building that housed foreigners! They'd welcome the respite from boredom in a capital where so little that was newsworthy ever happened. And the stories would go around the world.

"Tell me who it is, Sally. I need to talk to him."

She shook her head.

"Look, I think you were great not to tell the police his name. And I won't tell them either. I just want to find out if Mrs. Li caught up with him, if she was able to identify him. Don't you want to know if she reported him?"

"Oh no," she moaned.

"Come on, Sally. I'm on your side."

"His name is Shen Luo."

Janet remembered him. He was the least prepossessing of the students in the college, affecting the longish hair and hip manner of Western boys a couple of decades ago. Where had he found a model in Beijing where even audiotapes of Western songs were banned?

"Okay, just keep a low profile and don't say any more. Whether you tell or not, the worst that can happen to you is that you'll be sent home."

Her wail made Janet jump. Oh boy, Janet congratulated herself, for tact and counseling expertise you are the all-time champ!

One hour and three sherries later Sally was tucked up in bed snoring lightly, her unhappiness silent for a while.

15

Finally Janet was alone, everyone else's problem confessed, mulled over, and neatly minimized, while the list of suspects grew. Her mind began to pick again at the memory of what she had tried to do for Wang Qu Qing and how it might have jeopardized her own position.

The American embassy, providing service to American corporations, had distributed a flyer announcing the next date when the Educational Testing Service would be giving the English-language exam and the four cities where American proctors would administer it. The flyer announced, in the strident rhetoric of a TV commercial, that the test was open to any Chinese who paid the fee, that it was a test in the true democratic tradition: no special influence was needed to take it.

She had gone to the embassy to check it out. The woman at the reception desk was an Oriental American, as nasty to any Chinese who came through the door as someone could be who did not want to be identified with the native population. She wasn't particularly pleasant to Americans either. Not looking up from the paperback she was reading, she shoved a clipboard with signatures on it toward her.

Janet started to ask, "Can you tell me . . . ?"

"Sign the sheet."

"I just want . . ."

She looked up with a long-suffering expression on her face. "Everyone is supposed to sign the sheet."

Janet sighed. "Can you tell me whom I can see about something . . . ?"

"First door to your right."

"But I'm not sure . . ."

Her face went down again. She wasn't listening.

"Thank you so much," Janet said sweetly. "It's refreshing to have a touch of home when one is so far away."

She could have saved her sarcasm. The girl only grunted.

The first door on the right was open, and in the room sat five or six Chinese nationals at desks covered with papers and books. A man was typing at about two words a minute. No one paid any attention to her. She walked up to the first desk. "Can you help me?"

"Please?"

"I'd like to speak to someone about the English examination for Chinese students."

The woman turned to the man at the next desk and said something in Chinese. "You wish something?" he asked.

Janet smiled and pointed, then followed her finger through the half-open door of an inner office where a woman sat who looked like an American. A small frown creased her forehead when she saw Janet.

"Yes? Can I help you?"

"I have some questions about this flyer." She waved it in front of her.

The woman looked warily at her and reached for the paper. "Oh yes. We've been distributing them. May I have your name?"

"Janet Eldine."

She wrote it down. "Middle initial?"

"How many Janet Eldines were you expecting?" Politely curious.

Bridling, she asked, "Is there something you want to know about the TOEFL examination?" Before she could reply, the woman went on: "I've seen you here before, haven't I? In the library?"

Janet was somewhat mollified. It helped to be recognized, to be treated as if one really existed. "Yes," she said. "I've come several times to use your reference books."

"Most of our references have been turned over to Beijing University."

"Do you know it's virtually impossible for foreigners to use that library?"

"We just didn't have the room here."

I know, Janet thought. The embassy had at least six buildings on three different sites. And a new one was going up on a fourth site. Garbage expands to fit the space provided.

"Do you mind if I sit down?"

"What can I do for you?"

She sat. "The flyer says the English test is open to everyone, but the applicants need illegal American money to take it—unless the Chinese government pays for them. Isn't that a sort of catch-22?"

She giggled. "I guess so. We've tried to talk to the Educational Testing Service about it but they haven't responded to our communication."

"What's your position here?" Janet asked, curious.

"I'm the Assistant Cultural Attaché," she said in capital letters.

"Hm. Don't you think the flyer is misleading?"

She shrugged, disclaiming personal responsibility. "It didn't come over my desk."

"Is there someone who can tell me more about it?"

"What more is there to tell?"

"Well, I'd be curious to know why the embassy of the United States is party to a lie."

"Oh." She pursed her lips and put her palms out in protest. "It's not really a lie. And we are trying to get the regulation changed."

"When was the last time you were in touch with the ETS?"

She waved her hand vaguely. "I'm not sure . . . uh . . . six . . . seven months."

"What happens to the students who are barred from taking the test in the meantime?"

"Well, that's hardly our responsibility."

"But you're—we're—telling the Chinese people that the test is open to everybody."

It was clear that the Assistant Cultural Attaché was angry now.

"What would you say if I paid the fee for some students I know who want to take the test without government permission?"

She looked horrified. "Oh, that would be very unwise. The government would not look with favor . . ."

"Of course." Janet rose and left, not waiting to hear which government would not look with favor. The Assistant Cultural Attaché remained seated.

On the drive home from the embassy, she decided to solve the problem for Wang Qu Qing: she would send a check drawn on her American bank to the Educational Testing Service so that he could take the exam. Let's see what the Ministry of Education and the American embassy do about that!

Although she had heard nothing directly from either authority, the knowledge of what she had done might have got around at Beijing Xue Yuan. Mrs. Li had influential contacts in the ministry. Had the matter fueled her animosity toward foreigners—provided additional justification for not trusting them and for persuading some of the college administrators that this foreigner was fomenting rebellion among the students?

16

In a short time Mr. Guo was back again with an announcement. "Temple—very old. You will like to see."

"Now, Mr. Guo? This is hardly the time . . ."

"Very old. Government must make like new."

"An unrestored temple. That might be interesting. Are they working on it now?"

"Workers make like new."

She was curious to see how the ancient colors were applied to rebuilt beams. And she would like to get a close look at the scaffolding she had seen only from a distance that appeared to envelop a new building like an enormous, intricately woven basket. Maybe she could get some photographs to show her builder friends back home. "Okay," she said finally. "When can you arrange it?"

"All arranged," he told her. "We can go now."

She shook her head, marveling at the presumptuousness. He had been so certain that, just because he had decided she would go to see the temple, she would certainly go. "Right now?" The bureaucratic machinery rarely worked this quickly.

"Yes. We go."

"Isn't anyone else coming along?"

"This is for professor only. Special permission for professor."

She raised her eyebrows, skeptical at the implication that permission to see an old building being restored was such a singular honor. "Perhaps some of the other people would like to see it too." A couple of hours alone with Guo, listening to him mangle the English language, was not something she would willingly endure.

"No time." He hustled her into the waiting car. "No permission. Only professor."

And they were off to see the temple.

Catching sight of Sally on her way out, she tapped the driver's shoulder. But Sally looked meaningfully at Mr. Therefore and resisted the offer to visit another temple. "Thanks, but no, thanks. I'm just going to walk for a while—get the cobwebs out of my brain."

That would take some doing, Janet thought, and waved goodbye.

When the car stopped at the gate for its cursory inspection by the gatekeeper, the back door opened and Mrs. Li's husband got in. "I will ride with you," he said. From the front seat Mr. Guo looked at his father-in-law stonily and turned back to face the road.

Janet laughed and shook her head at the ways of the Chinese. "Where are you going?" she asked him.

"Where you are." He had lived long enough in the West to appreciate the situation, and he smiled a little. "You do not mind?" he asked belatedly.

She laughed again. "No, I don't mind. I'm glad you're here. I think we're on the way to a temple that's in the process of being rehabilitated."

"You think?"

"Communication is a sometime thing." She tried to answer cryptically so that Mr. Guo would not catch what she was saying. Jiao Zhong En got it and said something to Guo, who answered briefly.

"That's right—an old temple. The colors are being restored and my son-in-law thought you would be interested to see the process."

"Oh, good. And does it have the Chinese scaffolding on the outside?"

"Probably. We'll soon see. It's not far."

The driver pulled up to the right side of the wide street, at the foot of the building nestling like a fragile egg in its basket. There were no workmen visible. This was the hour of *wushui* and she wondered if they could get in before two. A small, fat woman sat on a crate at the entrance fast asleep, her head cradled in the carved wooden doorframe. Janet marveled at her ability to sleep so soundly sitting upright on a hard box. She had trouble sleeping in the soft reclining seat of a jet plane. But *wushui* was *wushui;* nobody wasted it.

They stepped over the foot-high threshold without waking the temple guardian. It took several minutes before their eyes adjusted and suddenly they could see the brilliance leap at them from the ceiling and the tops of columns. Gold threaded its way through the colors and she realized that it was not gold paint but gold leaf painstakingly applied. Flecks of it sparkled on the floor at the foot of one of the columns where a ladder stood leading up to scaffolding near the top. Against the wall was an enormous Buddha of some pale stone, chipped and marred by time. Perhaps by the weight of billions of prayers unanswered, dreams unfulfilled. A deep diagonal crack ran down the forehead and disappeared under the elongated left earlobe. She walked nearer to examine the base more closely, reaching out tentative fingers to touch the stone.

She was startled for a moment to hear what sounded like a handful of small pebbles—click-click-click—falling down the front of the sculpture, and she looked up through the network of bamboo, squinting into the dimness above. The Buddha loomed over her, smiling benignly. It was odd that such severely practical people as the current Chinese government should encourage the preservation —the reincarnation—of this broken god.

A giant hand at her back made her grunt and impelled her violently into the massive legs. For a crazy moment she thought she was being forced to kneel—atonement for the whimsical blasphemy she had been thinking. The click-click-click in her ears speeded up and grew into a roar, and something hit her face sharply.

An arm closed like a vise around her and flung her into the left-hand wall, knocking the breath out of her, slammed away from the god by an irate priest. The avalanche of splintering on the stone floor echoed around the sides of the room and made her flinch and cower against the wall. In the quiet aftermath, a hysterical woman's voice rose in rapid Chinese. Close to her ear she felt the heat of deep breath expired, and a man's voice undercut the hysteria with two firm words, and cut it off in mid-sentence.

Slowly she opened her eyes and looked into the face of Jiao Zhong En. "Are you all right?" The concern in his voice sounded forced— he got the words out with difficulty. She stared at him as if she didn't understand what she was hearing.

He untangled himself from her and helped her to her feet. The pain in her knee brought her out of it with a shock. "Ow!" She bent to look at the ugly scrape and fingered the edge of it, watching it ooze blood.

"That looks nasty," Jiao said. "We'd better get it cleaned up."

"What happened?"

He pointed up at the Buddha. Half its head was gone, and around the base were the splintered remnants of the ancient carving. Slowly her eyes went from the bottom to the top and realization hit her. "My God! I could have been killed!"

His mouth tightened and he put his arm around her shoulders. "Let's get out of here. Can you walk?"

"Yes, yes," she said impatiently. She wanted no coddling; she wanted to think.

Mr. Guo appeared suddenly, taking her other arm, and together they walked her to the entrance and lifted her out. For once Guo had nothing to say about the glories of ancient China. He looked as shaken as she felt. They might all have been seriously hurt if Jiao Zhong En didn't have such fast reflexes—and if Guo had not been somewhere out of range of the falling stone.

She frowned, but it wasn't with pain. Something she was trying to remember.

17

After dinner Janet sat in her room staring at the front page of the *China Daily* and the picture of the pretty Chinese peasant. Finally she became aware of the caption: "A beautiful Sichuan girl shows the beauty of labor—shouldering a heavy load of manure as she works in the countryside." Her eyebrows went up in disbelief.

She began to think about her near miss and remembered instead the visit of Mrs. Li's whole family. Yue Zhen had made a point of telling her that Jiao Zhong En had been at Mr. Xu's house the evening of the murder. Forthcoming of her, wasn't it? Somehow it sounded more significant than merely a daughter's resentment of her stepfather.

She tossed the paper aside and went to get Colette.

With the Frenchwoman protesting every step of the way, they followed the beam of the flashlight into the unfinished building. The cold dankness reached out and enveloped them as they made their way up the stairs. It was deathly silent.

This was not what she wanted to do, Janet thought. Her curiosity was purely cerebral; she did not want it luring her into dark buildings or other perilous situations.

"They will not be here," Colette whispered. "With the police everywhere, they will be afraid to stay."

"You're probably right. But where could they go?" If there was room available in homes of friends or relatives, there would be no need to live illegally in this place. In a park they could be questioned by anyone and be caught up in the maw of the bureaucracy and marked forever as people who had come to the attention of the authorities. But they might be sitting at desks in a dimly lit class-room working over their books as most students did every night after dinner. No one would question it if they stayed beyond the usual time.

Another flight of stairs. The flashlight played along the wall on the landing as Janet took the last step up. Suddenly she was sprawled on a world gone crazy. She grabbed for something solid and felt a head of hair before she was flipped away and over on her back. She sensed movement all around her—frantic scrabbling.

She sat up, trying to see through the darkness. Her flashlight was gone, and her scraped knee hurt again. She hoped it wasn't bleeding on her pants. All the writhing and falling had happened without a sound. The voice of Colette came through her confusion. "Sh! Sh! It is all right. It is Colette. Do not go. Do not go."

A tiny light came on at the level of the surface on which she was sitting with her legs out before her. Slowly her eyes started to register variations in the blackness and parts of faces and hands emerged. She jumped when, from right beside her, she heard some-one ask in Chinese what she was doing here.

"It is the professor," Colette answered in English. "She wishes to speak with you. She will tell no one you are here."

Another person spoke English. "Why does she speak with us?"

"She wishes to . . ."

Janet interrupted. "I'm sorry to invade your privacy. But when I heard that there were people living here, I had to ask you if you saw what happened outside your windows."

"There are no windows here. We put our beds outside the rooms so the light will not be seen."

"None of you goes sometimes to look out of a window?"

"We did not. We saw nothing."

A voice on her other side said quietly, "We sit here and talk. We do not need much light. Sometimes we sit in the dark."

She peered closely, trying to make out the features of the owner of the voice. "Colette said she saw something the night . . ."

"Yes, yes," Colette interjected quickly. "For a moment we were in the room. I did not stay at the window for long." The "we" must have been Colette and her friend.

"Do you think Mrs. Li knew you were here?"

No one answered.

"She came back to talk to the cook. Maybe at other times. She could have caught sight of someone—as I did."

The male voice spoke English again. "If she saw us, we know nothing of it. No cadre has come to talk about living here. No police."

If someone had come, Janet thought, it would have been too late then to kill Mrs. Li. Perhaps to prevent her telling, one of them had . . . "I'm sorry we bothered you. We'll go now. Please don't worry. I'll tell no one that you're here."

"I will stay a while." She felt Colette settling her back against the wall of the landing as she groped her way down the stairs.

18

Surprisingly, Jiao Zhong En was close behind her when she walked into the lobby. "I hope you do not mind my coming again so soon," he said.

"No, of course not. I'm glad you came."

"Is your leg all right?"

"It was nothing." She waved away his concern, uncomfortable because something about the incident still bothered her. "Lucky you were along."

"Lucky, yes. There is a scratch on your face." His fingers went out to touch it and she moved back.

"It's all right." Her own hand went up to her face.

"Guo, my . . . uh . . . son-in-law. He does not approve of Chinese who associate with foreigners, except for official purposes."

"And your purpose here is official?"

"Shall I say it is an opportunity for me to practice my English?" he said seriously. This was an officially acceptable reason for fraternization.

She laughed. "I don't think you can get away with that if you're ever questioned by the authorities. Your English is much too good."

"Without practice one forgets the nuances."

"Do you read much in English?"

"Yes, I do now. It was not possible for many years. It made people angry enough to see me read books in Chinese." Again he spoke quietly, matter-of-factly. With an undercurrent of sadness in his voice, but mostly just detachment.

"Where were you during the Cultural Revolution?" she asked.

"I stayed at the university most of the time. There were no students but the books were there."

"They didn't force you to go and work in the fields?"

"For years I was able to stay. Others went to the country. I would not." There was no change in his manner or his voice but she could feel the power of resistance in this man, the power of a gentle man who would submit to all things but the final indignity. "One day, when we thought the madness was done, a small band of Red Guards came to the campus. They took me with them."

His eyes looked away to the past. "They carried me to the south and left me. I was too . . . tired, perhaps, to move. There was nothing to do but work with the others. I learned how it is for peasants."

"It must have been very hard for you."

He looked back at her. "Have you seen peasants in the fields?"

She had. Everything was done by hand, the way it had been for thousands of years. Standing mid-calf in water, moving earth and water in buckets. And the odor—dear heaven! And these were the prosperous cooperatives, ten years after the Cultural Revolution.

"Did you meet your wife there?"

"No. She came to the university with other leaders. We talked. For a while, when she was there, I was not . . . uh . . . harassed."

"She didn't mind that you refused to go to the country with the others?"

"She did not like it. She tried to convince me that I should go. Then she left."

"Oh, you didn't marry then?"

"No. Some time later, I went south. It was not until five years ago that we met again here in Beijing. Then we married." He smiled briefly. "You know about me. Now I will ask about you."

"Okay." She grinned. "What do you want to know about me?"

"You have no children?" The population business kept coming up.

"I've never been married." A non sequitur, but quite logical to the Chinese, since extramarital sex not only immoral but illegal.

"You are not sad at this?"

"No, I never wanted children."

"How is that possible?"

"Aren't there people in China who choose not to have children?"

"There are some but they are not like you."

"Like me?"

"You like children, I think. I have seen you with some of the children here when I visit my friend."

"Oh, I like children well enough. It takes more than that to want your own."

She shrugged, bored with the subject. Too much responsibility for children before she was ready for it, that's what had turned her off marriage and family. An improvident father and a harried working mother and three younger brothers. But who cared now? It was all ancient history.

"You have no children of your own?" she asked him.

His mouth tightened. "To have a child is important. To care for you in your old age. To carry your name after you die. It is important."

She wanted to ask him why he hadn't married a younger woman if he so wanted a child. She didn't think it was because he was so in love with Mrs. Li. Was it because she was so "strong"? Had she bullied him into marriage? He was a lovely man but she thought he would be inclined to take the path of least resistance—in almost everything.

When she asked him if Mr. Guo and Yue Zhen had a good marriage he told her. The Chinese speak freely about matters that Westerners don't discuss with strangers, and even when they are confronted with foreigners they neither understand nor completely trust, they say nothing in response to a question rather than lie.

"Guo would be insulted if he heard me say this but he is a revolutionary with the soul of a mandarin," Jiao Zhong En said. "In his home his will rules. He decides what his small family should do, what they should say, how they should feel about every aspect of their lives. Just as the ancient mandarins imposed their will on others, so does he. They found their justification in tradition and convention, as well as in the power of their situation. He knows he is right because he does what is prescribed by the Party, by the cadres of his unit, by the precepts of Mao."

Guo sounded a lot like his mother-in-law, Janet thought. She must have been very fond of him.

Jiao Zhong En smiled a little and shook his head at Mr. Guo's impossible quest for perfection. "He wants to be the model Chinese worker. He . . . what is your expression? He walks a tightrope, struggling to keep his equilibrium. Yes, a perfect metaphor. It is a very difficult way he has set for himself. Policies change with the winds of economics, of international relationships, of such occurrences as an abundant wheat crop or the defection of a tennis player to the West. To express total commitment to every policy as it is announced and to live as if there had never been a completely contradictory one last week is a very difficult thing to do."

"Most of us in the West manage to do just that. In our newspapers, a foreign country may be an enemy one day and a good friend not so long after that. One day they believe the causes of crime lie in the manufacture and distribution of whiskey; another day it is uncaring parents, or a slow-moving justice system. One newspaper propounds a point of view and presents it as if it were indisputable fact, and other publications and media follow along, until the people believe there is no other viewpoint worth considering."

"I have seen this happen in other countries, yes. But here, every change of policy is official, and someone like Guo must make each change a part of his personal life, the way he makes friends, treats his wife, buys his food. Every suggestion a cadre makes is like an order given to him personally. It is too much."

"He's not a stupid person; he must be aware of the contradictions."

"Yes, he recognizes the absurdities and yet he is compelled to accept them as serious and good. That, I think, is what makes him so unhappy."

She listened to him talk, noticed the slowness and sweetness of his smile, the way his eyes met hers. She was very attracted to him. His calm, his detachment, acted as a soothing counterpoint to her own curiosity and involvement, her endless questioning. It might drive her crazy eventually, especially when things happened that cried out for involvement, but for now he made her sit back and relax, made her eyes stop snapping and become a little dreamy.

Before she knew she was thinking it, she said, "You were in the new building."

He caught his lower lip in his teeth and said nothing for a long time. Then: "Yes. I was there."

"I thought I recognized your voice." The significance of his presence there made her quiet now. She stared at him.

"I go there to speak with young friends." His voice was very low.

She couldn't ask him the obvious question, but when the silence had stretched for long moments, he told her. "I saw nothing."

She nodded. Would he say if he *had* seen something?

XING QI LIU—SATURDAY

1

When Janet turned the shower on in the bathroom Saturday morning she got hot water immediately. So there were those who did not agree with Mrs. Li's dictum that the hot water be reserved for those times when the foreigners were busy elsewhere.

Passing Laura Qian's door on the way back to her room she remembered again that she hadn't seen her for two days. In the United States, Janet would have feared either that Laura had been the victim of some kind of criminal attack or that she had decided to move elsewhere without letting anyone know. In China the conclusions foreigners jumped to were almost invariably linked to the mild to severe paranoia they suffered, living in what they viewed as a totalitarian country. Although she thought China might be more accurately described as a super-bureaucracy, her own dislike of petty officialdom made her almost as quick to suspect arbitrary behavior from government agencies. Now she had visions of Laura being taken away by the security police for heaven knew what trumped-up reason. Maybe being kept in an isolated cell, questioned unmercifully, even deprived of food to make her talk. About what? She had not got to that yet; she was still in the process of jumping to the conclusion. Because the Chinese attitude toward Chinese Americans was much more proprietary than it was toward other Americans, she hadn't had the same fears for Sally.

She dressed absentmindedly, wondering if she should ask Mrs. Hua, and give her more ammunition for nagging her cousin.

Her first breath of fresh air swept some of the worry from her mind. She always liked early mornings and this was a beautiful one, clear and cool and smelling of new trees. Perhaps because the air was mild, there was an illusion of spring. The trees and bushes in the small circle of carefully tended soil were wrapped in woven mats against the chill in the air, and outside the wooden gate masked workers swept the walks with huge bunches of twigs. Some said they hid their faces because they were ashamed of the menial work they did.

Already three or four men were practicing Tai Chi Chuan, moving with complete concentration through the stylized movements that once, in the distant past, were used to maim and kill. Now the arms came down slowly as in a dream of fighting and the bodies twisted in very slow motion to ward off imaginary blows. The older the people were, the more fluid the movements, the less dramatic the changes of stance. She saw one very old man pass his hands over his stomach, first one hand, then the other, while he stood with one leg forward and slightly flexed, his eyes fixed on the horizon. This exercise must be good for the bowels.

A very old woman sat on a bench watching a small child stumbling around. Women who did not work outside the home usually cared for a preschool child—doted on it. There were no dogs or cats in Beijing; small children got all the cuddling. Janet watched the baby for a while until he caught sight of her and ran to her. She picked him up, hoping he wouldn't take that moment to use the vent in his trousers. She smiled to the grandmother and carried him back to the bench, hugged him and patted his bare bottom in approval. Both women agreed this was a fine baby.

She walked down unpaved paths in front of apartment houses, some old, some recently built, where most of the faculty and married workers lived. Coming toward her was Wang Jun Xing, who was assistant to the college Principal. She attended Janet's lectures on American life every week and asked some very hostile questions. Her stereotype of Americans would have been funny if Janet had more tolerance of any kind of prejudice.

"Good morning," she said. "For whom are you looking?"

"I'm just taking a walk."

"It is very early in the morning."

Janet smiled. "The best time of day for walking—especially here."

"Why especially here?"

"Well, I live in a big city, like Beijing. It's always been a little frightening to walk in the city when there are no people around."

"Yes, American cities are not safe like Beijing. In China there are only a very few crimes."

"Maybe." Or maybe you think that because the *Renmin Ribao* doesn't report crimes the way American newspapers do. Some of the women she'd met had warned her about holding on to her purse on Wangfujing—just as women warned each other in Philadelphia. But she didn't want to start the day with an argument. "We can talk more about this at the lecture next week."

"You would like to come to my house for tea?"

"Why . . . uh . . ."

"I live here." She pointed to the building they were standing in front of. "You are welcome."

"Why, thank you. I'd like that." She was interested in visiting a Chinese home and she might, at the same time, mend some fences, convince Wang Jun Xing that the United States had things to recommend it.

The apartment consisted of a small kitchen and a living room–bedroom. She could see a toilet through a half-open door, but no bathing fixtures. All those who lived in the compound went to the community showers, the use of which was strictly limited to twice a week in semi-arid Beijing.

Janet sat in the single easy chair facing the double bed, which was neatly made up, the brocade quilt folded at the foot, the pillow at the head covered with a terry-cloth hand towel. Crowded into the room were an ordinary wooden chair, three small square stools, and a glass-fronted bookcase in which she could see such unlikely mates as Dickens's *David Copperfield* and a lurid paperback thriller, both, of course, in English. There were no lurid thrillers in Chinese. Right next to the bookcase on a small chest of drawers was an ornate clock, carefully draped with a dustcloth. The small round table at her elbow was probably where the family ate their meals, seated on the space-saving stools. Perhaps that was why the Chinese spent so little social time at meals; sitting on a backless stool did not encourage lingering at the table.

Jun Xing came in with tea. "This is not as beautiful as the houses in your country." She was always this way with Janet—aggressive in a way that made it clear that she expected attack.

"I was thinking that this is very nice," Janet lied. "That's a beautiful clock."

"Thank you." She lovingly rearranged the dustcloth.

Wang Jun Xing, with the welcoming party at the airport, had given no indication that she spoke English. Probably her hostility toward Americans and her disapproval of permitting them to teach Chinese students. Was she one of those who had sided with Mrs. Li to protest that she was spoiling the young people?

"Last week you talked about families in America."

"Yes. Is there a question you didn't get a chance to ask?"

"I think parents in America do not love their children."

Some question.

"The children leave home and live apart. They must earn money and pay for rent and food."

"Many young people do that because they want to be independent, make their own decisions."

"They do not respect their parents."

"That's not it. We just believe that people should learn to make decisions and profit from their mistakes."

"The parents want this?"

"Most parents see the value of this."

"Chinese families stay together."

They don't have a helluva lot of choice, thought Janet, looking around the small apartment that housed two adults and two children. It would be many years before the number of buildings erected in China was sufficient to house the generations separately.

"We believe that families can be close even if they don't live in the same house."

"Children in America do not honor their parents."

Okay. Next question.

She noticed a small snapshot under the glass that covered the table. "Is this your family?"

"My relatives from America. They visited here this year."

"Oh, you have family in America! Where do they live?"

"In Ohio." She said it carefully, a difficult word. "In the city of Cleveland."

"Really! Would you like to visit them?"

"I do not like. I will not have permission to go to America. Only people who must study for the future of China will go abroad."

"Who knows what will happen in five or ten years? Six years ago, I stood on the border of China in Hong Kong and was not permitted to cross over. Today many foreigners are invited. The world changes—sometimes very quickly."

Jun Xing shook her head impatiently, as if this was not even to be considered. If something is not permitted, you don't wish for it. You don't even bother speculating about it. Janet had encountered this attitude with her students too, because their future had been determined for them. "Since the Cultural Revolution," one of them had said, "I do not let my mind think of such things."

But for many of them, after class it was a different story altogether. In private they confided wishes and dissatisfactions to her quite freely. They were as frank—and as dissatisfied—as young Americans.

Wang Jun Xing, of course, would not be so candid with a foreigner. Janet wondered if she had suffered during the Cultural Revolution because she had relatives in America. She had heard of others who had been persecuted as "running dogs of capitalists" because they had relatives abroad.

"Did your relatives enjoy visiting here?" she asked.

"Yes. They do not like America very much."

"Do they want to come back to China to stay?"

She said nothing.

When Janet got up to leave, she told her, "My home is always open to you. I hope you will come again."

"Thank you. I'd like to."

"You will come for dinner." She proffered the invitation as aggressively as she was uncivil about Americans. Maybe it was just a mannerism. Maybe she was not as hostile as she sounded.

2

Janet stopped at the door to the dining room and watched through the glass. Masomakali, the cook, and several of the kitchen men whispered in a corner. Masomakali's gestures were agitated, his voice going up before he let it drop again. Apparently, being frightened of the police hadn't interfered with their business dealings.

When she pushed the door open, the group broke up and Masomakali joined her at the counter. "Good morning to you!" His cheerfulness was strained. "How are you this morning?"

"Fine, thank you. How are you?"

He held his hand out palm down and tipped it down one side and then down the other, in a gesture that indicated so-so. "It is China, you know." He laughed. "It is the way it is."

She smiled sympathetically.

They finished the unappetizing breakfast quickly. It seemed that hot water would be the only improvement in the building. Masomakali laconically waved her out. "Enjoy your teaching."

The mail had arrived—the American mailman went through sleet and hail, but Chinese mailmen got up at five in the morning. Letters were propped up against the glass of the doorman's cubicle, address side out. She put her hand through the opening and took the one addressed to her.

Struggling to open the envelope, she stepped out of the doorway. Chinese envelopes required more than a casual lick of the tongue before being mailed. Each envelope was carefully sealed with a brush and strong glue, right up to the corners, so that not even a knife could be inserted. She tried to tear the end off without ruining the letter inside. Whom did she know in China to send her letters? She fussed with it as she walked.

The fifteen-foot chalkboard at the side of the path had a new message on it, and for a moment she forgot the half-opened envelope. Borders decorated with birds and flowers were charming and skillfully done, and pink and yellow and green chalks made the Chinese text even more attractive to the foreigner's eyes. It reminded her of what someone had once said about Times Square: If one had never learned to read, the neon signs would be breathtakingly beautiful.

Finally she had the letter out of the envelope, a long tear in it where it had caught in the impervious glue. It was a note from Laura saying that she had moved near her new job. It had all been very sudden. She was in a workers' compound that had two floors of a building set aside for overseas Chinese, and those who committed themselves to a long time in China had been promised new apartments shortly. The note hinted in very colloquial English that she had better not say too much in a letter.

Foreigners working in China were convinced that their letters were routinely opened by government officials, seeing as proof envelope flaps obviously resealed and letters delayed. Although how anyone could get into the envelopes and reseal them was a mystery.

Laura's letter sounded as if something was troubling her but didn't say so clearly. Only that she *hoped* she *would be able* to see her soon. The words were underlined as if to convey more than was said.

Mrs. Hua must have more information and as soon as her class was over she would demand to be told where the American woman was.

3

She avoided the side entrance to the classroom building. Passing the toilets with the overpowering stench of urine that followed one up the staircase to the third floor was just too much to take in the morning. She was reminded fleetingly of subway entrances at home. Inside the front door a worker was swabbing the lobby with a mop dipped in cold water that gave off its own distinctive odor.

Saturday was just another weekday in China and in the classroom students were busily washing the desks and chalkboards. One was kicking up a royal dust, carefully sweeping the dirt and bits of trash into the corner. The others crowded around her, friendly, happy to see her. One moved a chair up for her to sit in, another took the books and papers from her arms and put them on the table at the front of the room. She grinned, just as happy to be with them again.

They said nothing about the murder, as if, now that they had delegated the responsibility to her, they could get on with the business of their lives.

Today Janet had planned to give them some experience in practical communication. She went next door to an office she shared with a teacher of French who had no students. He sat from early morning until late afternoon bent over French grammars and dictionaries, murmuring to himself the declensions and conjugations. He really came alive only when Mrs. Hua had time away from her many duties —and the four students of French still left in the college—to sit and speak with him. In China, Russian was dead and French was at its last gasp.

From the drawers of her desk she took out articles of clothing she had stored in preparation for today's lesson, hangers, and a folder of photographs of department store counters, haberdashers, and specialty shops. She was going to take her class on a shopping spree.

Two of them were already at the door of the office to see if she needed help, smiling in anticipation. This English class was so different from anything they were accustomed to with their serious Chinese professors who sat on their dignity and lectured to them hour after hour.

In the classroom Janet placed two chairs with backs facing about four feet apart. On them she rested a pole she had commandeered from an undusted corner of the Foreign Students Building, and hung the clothing on the pole to simulate a rack in a store. On chairs and desks near the rack she put belts and socks and sweaters, while the students gathered around laughing and questioning and naming the items they had words for.

For the next two hours they talked about stores and shopping, purchased pants and sweaters and socks, discussed sizes and lengths and widths, talked about trying things on, asked about the belt on the counter (not *under* the counter!), and managed to have a good time even while they struggled with the language. She came away exhilarated, feeling successful, as she always did after teaching.

4

When it was over she met Mrs. Hua and they walked together back to the Foreign Students Building.

"I want to see Laura," Janet said without preamble.

"She lives near her work now." Mrs. Hua smiled.

"I want to go there. Where is it?"

"These things must be arranged." Her soft smile did nothing to alleviate Janet's escalating worry about Laura. At the same time, her abrupt directness in the face of Mrs. Hua's gentle temporizing made her feel like a hulking, awkward clod, blundering in an almost physical sense.

"Arrange it, then, Mrs. Hua. I want to go there tomorrow."

"I do not know if it is possible."

"I see no reason why it should not be possible for me to visit my friend. I want to see her tomorrow, or I'll go to the authorities and make my own arrangements." Cousin or no cousin, Laura was a foreigner in China.

"Laura will come here soon. She has clothes yet in her room."

"I don't want to wait. I want to see her, Mrs. Hua." A sudden thought struck her. "Was Laura here on Thursday?"

"Thursday? No. I do not think so. You mean on Thursday, when Mrs. Li was murdered?"

"No, no. I don't mean . . . Laura couldn't . . ."

"What does she have to do with this?" The voice of Comrade Hua was sharper than she had ever heard it. Janet met her narrowed eyes. She looks suspicious, Janet thought. Is it me she doesn't trust or does she know something about the murder? The thoughts were a counterpoint to her concern for Laura.

"You misunderstand, Mrs. Hua," she said.

"I thought you said . . ."

"That policeman is looking at us, Mrs. Hua."

Mrs. Hua nodded to the PLA man standing near the cubicle in the lobby of the Foreign Students Building. He ignored her and grumped something at Janet. She turned inquiringly to Mrs. Hua, who, with her customary placating smile, whispered, "He says you had a fight—no, argued—with Mrs. Li. He asks what the argument was."

"We've been all over that with the officer in charge. Does every man here conduct his own investigation? You can tell him. You know what we argued about."

She spoke to the soldier, softly, probably making it all sound unimportant: She had had a disagreement with a penny-pinching hotel manager. It happened all the time without murderous consequences. He continued to stare at her from under ferocious brows, but his unlined skin and rosy peasant cheeks removed the menace from the glare. Janet grinned at him. He didn't grin back.

Finally he turned away and began to speak to the old doorman. Some workers from the other buildings listened, enthralled by the exchange, and, as it went on and on, added their own opinions and observations. Apparently she was no longer wanted here, but when she started to leave the soldier moved to block her path. Like policemen everywhere, he felt that those involved in an investigation were obliged to sit and wait until somebody got around to thinking of another question.

"Will you tell him, please, Mrs. Hua, that if they have anything more to say to me, I'll be in my room."

"I will tell him that you are old and very tired," she said helpfully. Old, indeed. She sometimes got the feeling that she was aging geometrically instead of chronologically. They were always asking her how old she was and helping her up and down curbs and telling her at all hours of the day that she should "have a rest." She clomped into her room and just missed slamming the door.

Sitting in the plastic easy chair, she felt the cold rise from the stone floor and the shiny plastic to fill her bones. Why was she so worried about Laura? It must be just the whole atmosphere of murder and suspicion. . . . She shivered.

5

A few minutes later there was a knock and she opened the door to see two PLA men and Chang. "Ask you," he said to her, pointing to the soldiers.

She opened the door wider and motioned them inside. The three of them were looking at her—with curiosity? suspicion? stolid disinterest? The only thing she was sure of was that Chang was smiling and the soldiers were not.

"You find old woman Li," Chang started, and then waited expectantly.

Aw, hell, she thought. Eldine's Law again: Nothing ever settles anything. "No, I did *not* find her. I knew nothing about it until I was told the police had been called!" She spoke slowly with exaggerated emphasis.

"You see there." He pointed at her door to indicate the side of the building opposite to where her room was located.

"I walk there. I have a friend who lives nearby."

Chang smiled and nodded, then spoke at length to the soldiers. When he was finished, he asked her, "Why?"

She looked at him, puzzled.

"Li. You find. Why?"

She shook her head. "I went to visit a friend in the building next to this one. Outside the back gate. A friend. In that building." She pointed through her door to the other side.

He smiled and nodded and again spoke to the soldiers. She didn't hear the word for friend—*pengyou*. Strongly suspecting that they had reached the limit of his understanding of English with the words "find" and "why," she wondered what he was saying to them, what he was attributing to her.

The soldiers seemed to lose interest as he went on and on. Nodding to her while he was still talking, they left. The little man looked comically disappointed, with his mouth still open on an uncompleted word. His time in the limelight was over. As she closed the door behind them she could hear him talking again, but the soldiers were still saying nothing.

What now? she thought. Were they slowly and inexorably building a case against her in spite of Mrs. Hua's good offices and her own denials that she had found the body?

She stood in the middle of the room for a few minutes, frowning, then locked the door behind her and went to look for Mrs. Hua. She couldn't find her but she did see Colette and Ka Ka Chi sitting alone in the dining room looking gloomy. "Sorry to interrupt." Her apology was perfunctory. She was too concerned about her own position to make much of the amenities. "Do you know," she demanded, "that people are saying *I* found her?!"

"Oh no," Ka Ka Chi said. "The old man who guards the door found her. Everyone knows this."

"Chang just brought a couple of PLA men in to ask me what I was doing out there. I'm pretty sure he was saying I found her, and that I didn't tell anyone about it."

"He knows this is not so. He is not right in the head."

"*Did* you find her?" Colette asked. "If I had found her I would tell no one—no one!"

"Certainly not! Why would I keep it a secret? For that matter, why would you?"

"It would mean questions, questions! Perhaps, even, they would take one to prison. It is best to say nothing."

"For goodness' sake, Colette, anyone could have stumbled on her body! That doesn't make a person suspect."

"You think not? Wait! You will see for yourself."

Janet shrugged. "Let's take a walk," she said. She felt the need for air, the need to get away from the soldiers and the questioning, the uneasiness in everyone's eyes. "I'll get Sally, okay?"

But before they could leave, Laura Qian came in. "Laura! You're back!" Standing in the corridor, the women hugged each other. Janet herded them all into her room.

"Laura, what happened to you? We were so worried!" She felt guilty that she had thought even for a moment that Laura might have had something to do with Mrs. Li's death.

"They said I couldn't stay here any longer—didn't even give me time to get my things together."

"But why?"

"Dear old Comrade Li, of course! She wouldn't let me live here after I got another job. She went on and on about it until the Principal said I'd have to move to the unit where I work."

"But I thought you wanted to move from here."

"What I wanted was to live alone—someplace without guards and doormen. But that's not possible."

"Why did it matter to Mrs. Li? There are plenty of empty rooms."

"She thought I ought to be with other overseas Chinese—maybe where I could be watched even more closely."

"And Mrs. Hua agreed?"

"I think she just went along to avoid trouble. She said something about being responsible for me, with my parents so far away. Can you imagine that, treating me as if I were one of the students! Ooh, I could have killed that Li!"

"Well," Sally said, "somebody sure did."

"What?"

"Well, she didn't stab herself."

Laura began to shake. "S-s-stab . . . ooh . . . ooh . . ." She had jumped up and now she began to tremble. The shaking seemed to take the strength from her legs and she sank to the floor, huddling with her head down. The sound of her teeth raised goose bumps on Janet's arms. Was it shock at hearing about murder so suddenly or was it a delayed reaction to murdering someone? Janet took a gulp of the sherry right from the bottle before she poured some for Laura, but she was afraid to put the glass to the girl's mouth, afraid her chattering teeth would bite right through it.

This beautiful, delicate young woman strangling someone and then . . . Nonsense!

She got the towel hanging from the hook on the hat tree and wet it with water from the carafe. Laura's trembling stopped and she took the towel and patted her face with it.

"Thanks," she said into the towel. "I don't know what hit me."

"Gee, I'm sorry, Laura. I didn't mean it. I thought you knew about Mrs. Li." Sally appeared contrite, but she peered intently at Laura, also wondering at the intensity of her reaction.

"When did it happen?"

"Sometime Thursday night. She was found yesterday morning, out back."

"Who could have done such a terrible thing? Most of the people in the building are her old comrades. They have the iron rice bowl here. And she was satisfied that they were satisfied. Only the foreigners had trouble with her."

The door flew open and Mrs. Hua stood there. "Laura! They told me you were here!"

Mrs. Hua had probably been in her office at the other end of the compound. Who had taken the trouble to inform her that her cousin had come into the building? And why had she dashed here, obviously upset?

She saw Janet and Sally staring at her and recovered somewhat her conventional manner. She smiled sweetly and explained, "I heard Laura was here. I wanted to know how she was getting along in her new place. Is everything all right, Laura?" The smile could not completely cover the worried frown.

"I'm fine. Everything is all right." Laura was pale but composed again.

"And your new work? It is also all right?"

"Yes, I prefer it to teaching. I like translating for the bank. But I work much longer hours."

"And you eat with the workers?"

"No. I've arranged with a friend to share her meals. I pay for my food and help with the shopping and cooking. Then we eat in her apartment with her husband and son."

"That is very nice. I am happy you have friends close by."

"I preferred it here." Laura spoke stiffly, remembering that her cousin had sided with Mrs. Li.

"Yes, yes. But you know you could not live here if you did not work in the college any longer."

"Oh, you don't have to pretend with me! There are people living in the compound who don't work here. And this building is practically empty. Even when there's a meeting, only the upper floors are used. I could have stayed if it weren't for Mrs. Li."

"And why the big hurry to get Laura out?" Janet asked. "Without letting her friends here know she was going?"

Mrs. Hua's lips tightened but she said nothing. There was probably nothing to say. Decisions were made by those in authority and people were bound by those decisions. There was no obligation to discuss changes in advance or to give people time to prepare for them. The Chinese, by and large, accepted that. Or at least lived by it. That was just the way things were.

They all heard the phone ring in the cubicle down the hall. It seemed a long time before the old man knocked on the door to tell

Janet that the call was for her. She beat him back to the cubicle and picked up the red phone. "Hello?"

"Professor Aldane?"

"Yes?"

"Mr. Guo here."

"Yes, Mr. Guo. What is it?"

"What? Mr. Guo here."

"Mr. Guo, yes. This is Dr. Eldine. Did you want to tell me something?"

"Yes, Professor Aldane. You told to me you are wanting to visit library, yes?"

A stillness came over her. "No, Mr. Guo," she said quietly. "I do not want to visit the library—or any other place." A vision of the cracked Buddha swam before her eyes and her knee began to ache. "I think I'd better rest for a while."

"I try to get permission. I have friend in office of ministry. He tries to get permission. Hello? Hello? Professor Aldane?"

"Yes, Mr. Guo, I'm still here. I don't want to visit the library."

"If I do not have friend in ministry it is very *difficile* . . ."

The line went dead. Trouble on the telephone line was very common. She hung up.

Of course, arranging visits was his job. It was not his fault that all this murder business took away the desire for sightseeing.

The women sat on the bed and two chairs in Laura's room while she packed the things she had left behind. Sally, "helping" her by rummaging in the drawers and backpack, suddenly gasped. Slowly she drew her hand out of the backpack and displayed the knife she grasped by the handle.

There was a breath-holding silence while everyone stared at the knife and at Sally. Janet could read her mind. Mrs. Hua probably could, too. Laura just looked puzzled. "What's the matter?" she asked.

"Huh? Oh . . . uh . . . nothing. Nothing's the matter. I just found this knife."

"Yeah, that's a knife. I use it to peel apples."

Everyone was cautioned to peel fruit because of the heavy spraying with insecticides. The parks and picnic grounds were always strewn with lengths of apple peel.

It was a very large knife for peeling apples.

Sally nodded but she continued to clutch the knife as if she were ready to hold off an attacker. Laura put her hand out and slowly she relinquished it. Mrs. Hua and Janet started to talk at the same time and laughed—and the uncomfortable moment was over.

So this was what it was like to live in a house where a murder had been committed, Janet thought.

6

After Laura had gathered up her belongings Mrs. Hua went back to work and the others rode bikes down to the center of the city. Bicycles went in both directions on the narrow road, most of the riders leaning precariously over to smile at the Western women. A man made his way pulling a cart piled high with baskets. A horse-drawn wagon rolled leisurely through the banks of cyclists.

They rode over a hilly rise out of the dust onto the main highway that took them into the city. This was a four-lane road, extraordinarily wide when one considered that there were almost no cars. It was edged by new concrete guardrails and the effect was clean and bright and new. The newness fitted in with the miles of buildings going up several hundred feet in from the guardrails on both sides. For a while, the basketwork scaffolding would mask the ugliness of the concrete blocks.

Between large office buildings and buildings in progress were fields being tilled by hand, surprisingly close to the center of this modern capital. They passed the Beijing Hotel, where they sometimes went to browse in the lobby's gift and souvenir shops and have a drink or ice cream. The hotel where Sally said she had met her friend. A lounge had recently been furnished on the rooftop and the resident foreigners had already begun to congregate there on mild evenings, an alternative to the International Club on embassy row.

A turn to the left after the hotel and they were on Wangfujing, packed storefront to storefront with people strolling in both directions. A car plowed through them honking incessantly and the people turned, smiling, and strolled out of the way. It was all amazingly good-natured. Janet loved it—the smiles, the curious looks, the sounds of Chinese spoken all around her.

They checked their bikes with a street attendant and became part of the crowd as they worked their way to the beautiful little chop shop that created seals out of stone, onyx and marble carvings of lions, dogs, and mandarins. Janet planned to have one made for herself and several to take back to Philadelphia for friends. It would be fun to spend an hour sometime with the friendly saleswoman deciding how to translate Western names into Chinese characters.

It spoiled Janet's pleasure having to pretend that she wasn't thinking about the knife in Laura's bag.

They moved along toward Beijing's only department store, trying to look at the shopwindows while they adroitly avoided the sharp elbows of the people who wanted to pass them. They could be mortally gored if they were not careful—but never with malice. It was just a way of getting through the crowds. Most of the windows were streaked and dusty. No effort had been made to make them attractive or even to display fairly the merchandise being sold inside. To Western eyes it seemed a commercial opportunity lost.

She turned to the person beside her, who seemed to be getting closer than was necessary—even on Wangfujing. "Wang Qu Qing!" She laughed. "Are you following us?"

"Yes. I see you leave. I follow on my bicycle." He seemed very proud of what he had done.

"Why did you follow us?"

He smiled and shrugged. Just a whim.

"We're going to the store."

"I will go too."

He fell in with them, steering his bike casually through the press of people. Her mind jerked once more to the murder and a thought occurred to her. "Do you know Mrs. Li's husband?"

"Yes."

"Did you see him Thursday?"

"Yes."

"At the Foreign Students Building?"

"Yes. I was there to visit my friends. Then I practice English with you."

"What time were you there?"

"I come over *wushui.* Professor Jiao Zhong En is there."

"Over *wushui?*"

"After *wushui.*"

"What time did you leave for dinner?"

"I do not leave. My friend Petiri has much to eat from Friendship Store. We eat sausage rolls."

"How long were you in your friend's room?"

"Not long."

"At what time did you see Professor Jiao?"

"We are practicing English. I see him leave at gate. Soon everybody leaves."

The group usually broke up a little before seven.

"You didn't see him before that?"

"No. Not before."

His wife had probably been dead by then.

"How about Mr. Guo? Was he there too?"

He shook his head. He had not seen Mr. Guo—or he did not remember.

7

"You can ask if Guo came to Foreign Students Building. I will take you."

"Take me where?"

"To the house of Guo. It is not far."

She thought for only a second. "I'll see you all back at dinner," she said, and grabbed the boy by the arm before he could start talking and hustled him down the narrow street toward which he had pointed. They walked quickly and she was soon lost in the turnings. Low houses blackened with centuries-old soot showed their backs and walls to the cobbled streets. He led her down a dark alley that opened suddenly into a small four-sided courtyard. Baby carriages, earthenware jugs, old cooking pots, cluttered it. Four doors opened into houses from which delicious food smells emanated.

"Here is Guo's house. We go in." And he entered one of the doors without knocking before Janet could stop him. She followed slowly, stopping on the threshold to wait for an invitation.

Mr. Guo rose from the wooden table in the corner of the room looking stunned. "Professor Aldane! You are here!"

Janet grinned weakly. "Mr. Guo, I hope you don't mind. We . . . er . . . were passing by."

Wang Qu Qing began to chatter. God knew what he was saying. "Wang Qu Qing! Wang Qu Qing!" He stopped abruptly.

"I say you want to ask him questions," he protested indignantly.

"Yes, that's what I thought you were saying."

Guo dazedly pulled out the other chair for her, while Wang Qu Qing squatted against the wall looking from one to the other expectantly.

"It's nothing important, Mr. Guo." Already it all seemed too important—searching out the man, invading his house. "Uh, where is Yue Zhen?" She was still trying to make it sound like a casual visit.

He looked at her as if he didn't understand.

"Your wife? Is she at work?"

"Wife? She goes to child."

Wang Qu Qing saw her confusion and explained. The baby was cared for by a great-aunt while the couple was at work. Yue Zhen had gone to bring him home.

"How is your father feeling, Mr. Guo? Is he better?"

"Father? Yes, he is well."

"Oh, good. He must have been happy to see you."

He said nothing.

"Last week. When you went to his house."

"I was to Shanxi Province, yes."

She nodded. "Er . . . When did you get back to Beijing?"

"In Shanxi Province one week." He was still dazed at the unexpected visit, but he was beginning to rally. "You are warmly welcome to my poor house."

"Oh, thank you, Mr. Guo. It's a lovely house."

"No," he said. "My wife will make tea soon. Soon she comes."

"We can't stay, Mr. Guo. Your good friend, the cook, will be very angry if I don't get back in time for dinner," she added fatuously.

"Yes, good friend. Friend to old Li. Walked Long March. Friends."

Janet nodded. Good friends—perpetually at each other's throat. "Well, I'm glad you're back, Mr. Guo. I'll see you in class on Monday. We missed you, you know. What day did you say you got back?"

Wang Qu Qing intervened, translating rapidly. Maybe Guo would chalk up the question to the kind of intrusiveness teachers were often guilty of.

"Friday," she heard him answer.

"Friday? I'm sure I saw you at the Foreign Students Building on Thursday, Mr. Guo. Late in the afternoon, I think."

Wang Qu Qing translated again. Guo turned from him to look at her a little wildly. Janet was beginning to think that this unexpected event in his life was just too much for him to handle. He was a very rigid young man.

"He returned home Friday in the morning." Janet looked up to see that Yue Zhen had come quietly into the room with the baby in her arms.

Janet nodded cheerfully. "Well, then, I was mistaken. No harm done!" She smiled at Yue Zhen absently, remembering that she had not been in class either. That was unusual. "Were you sick, Yue Zhen?" she asked. "You weren't in class all last week either."

"I was to hospital. For operation."

"I hope it was nothing serious. Are you all right now?" Stupid of me, Janet thought, not to have remembered about her absence before this. But she hadn't said a thing about being in the hospital.

"I am fine. You know, I have one child. One family, one child."

"Oh." Janet realized what the operation was.

"I did not want this operation. Now I will never have child."

Not just abortion. She had been sterilized.

"Couldn't you refuse to have the operation?"

"It is my duty. I have one child."

"Did you want to have more children?"

"If something happens to my child, my husband and I will have no family. My brother has three children. He is peasant. Three children!" She looked at her husband. He sat staring into the distance.

"How did your husband feel about it?" she asked, lowering her voice unconsciously. She didn't think he would hear if they were shouting.

"He wants. He . . ." She interrupted herself. "My mother would be very angry if I did not have operation. It is my duty to my country."

"What could she do if you refused?"

"She would speak against me. Perhaps I must wait more years for good place to live, for bicycle." Her head was bowed. Her hands in her lap tore at each other. Her words were those of resignation but her hands expressed fury. Here was another person who hated Mrs. Li.

"When did you leave the hospital, Yue Zhen?"

"I went home on Thursday but I was not able to come to class."

"No, no. Of course not." Just how sick was she when she got home? "Did you see your mother on Thursday at all?"

There was a long pause. Then: "No. I do not see her." She seemed to be reverting back to her careful preparation of each English sentence before she went public with it.

8

It was a long bike ride home, and even Wang Qu Qing had to keep his eyes on the dinner-hour traffic, so there was time to think. The cook must have heard her tell the officer that she had seen Mr. Guo on Thursday and repeated it to Guo. The sound of the rock falling from the Buddha almost made her lose control of the bike. Was it just chance that Guo's father-in-law had come along to the temple?

She was very sorry that she had gone to Guo's house.

Back home, Janet nodded curtly to the cook, as he did to her. He looked like the textbook heart-attack case. Not the physical Type A that she'd always visualized as the tall, handsome, red-faced workaholic. He was of medium height and really fat. He waddled when he walked. She would watch him eat, shoveling the rice into his mouth and stuffing greasy meat after it. His face always shone with grease, as if he had been oiled inside and out. The fat seemed to interfere with his breathing; his words came out on breathy gasps, as if he had just been running. And the inevitable dirty wet cigarette always hung from the corner of his mouth. A very unattractive person.

What a relief it would be if it turned out that he was the murderer. She was getting more and more uncomfortable about the motives and feelings being uncovered; she didn't want to discover that one of her friends had murdered Mrs. Li.

XING QI TIAN—SUNDAY

1

Sunday, Janet made a list of the questions that needed answering:

1. Had anyone seen Mrs. Li's husband with his wife on Thursday?
2. How did Mrs. Li and her husband get along? Was it a reasonably good marriage?
3. Had anyone seen Yue Zhen around the building on Thursday?
4. Could Mr. Guo have raised a hand against Mrs. Li? She answered this immediately: No. She may have been his mother-in-law but she was also a cadre. He was too authority-ridden, too upwardly mobile. She giggled as she wrote. No Chinese sociologist would admit such a concept in China!

Unhappy as Guo might be about the sterilization of his wife, he was too loyal a party member to resist a mandate. Anyhow, he had been miles away on Thursday.

5. Had Laura come back Thursday to get her things and had she got into a fight with Mrs. Li?
6. What about the African students? What had they been doing when Mrs. Li was murdered? Ka Ka Chi had had nothing much to do with her. Masomakali did drugs and was not always rational. Maybe he had been provoked into violence. Haji hated the food; he had once sent a plateful of it flying across the dining room to smash against the wall. But he seemed more angry with the cook than with Mrs. Li. Anyway, he was rarely around. If he had been in the compound on Thursday someone might have noticed him.
7. And what about the cook? Maybe he had been sick because he had just killed her, not merely found her by accident. Maybe his fear of exposure was too great to risk letting her live, even though he had some hold over her. If Mrs. Li had talked to the others about him there might be some clue to how far he could be pushed before he got violent. Chang might be a good person to question. He and the cook didn't get along; he might be willing to talk.
8. The doorman and Chang? Chang was simple but he didn't

appear to be violent. On the contrary, he was easily frightened off at the threat of violence. The old man was Mrs. Li's friend. So were the maids and bookkeepers.

9. The students, Mr. Xu—about ten people had gathered Thursday night. Any one of them could have wandered away and then come back again. But surely none of the students had motive strong enough for murder. Mr. Xu could still be carrying around his hatred of her.

10. The people living in the unfinished building. Had Mrs. Li represented a threat to those who were breaking the law? Would such a small violation as trespass cause fear enough to result in murder?

11. And then there was Sally and her student. Could fear of disclosure have sent one of them to reason with Mrs. Li—with a Mrs. Li who accepted no reason but the state's?

12. How about Mrs. Hua, whose relationship to Laura might have precipitated contention? Laura's emotional reaction could have been horror at the realization that her cousin was a murderer.

She threw her pen down and grabbed her padded jacket. As she had told her students, she was better at asking questions than she was at answering them.

2

Before she could get out, there was someone at the door. She opened to Ching Mei, Dawang, and Zhu Mei, three undergraduates who came regularly to the evening sessions to practice English. Welcoming them in, she noticed that Ching Mei seemed jittery. Janet drew her into the room and urged her to sit in one of the easy chairs. Dawang and Zhu Mei sat on the stools against the wall.

"Are you feeling well, Ching Mei?"

She looked to Dawang for translation but Janet interceded. *"Ni hao ma?"* she asked. "How are you?"

"I'm fine," the girl answered. But it was obvious that she was not very well.

Her friends looked at her anxiously and Zhu Mei told Janet, "She remembers her mother. Some days she is afraid, as in the past."

The older woman put her arm around Ching Mei and held her

close. Once before, her world had been destroyed, so it was not surprising that there were days when she was anxious and nervous.

Ching Mei said something to Dawang, who translated. "She says the murder of Comrade Li makes her again afraid."

"Did she know Mrs. Li before she came to Beijing?"

"No, she does not know her. Her family lives in Guangzhou. She knows only that Li is terrible woman. Like those who disgrace father and shame mother."

Could this child have murdered a woman she thought was terrible —like those who had ruined her family? It was not conceivable that she would spend time planning cold-bloodedly to kill a woman who was some kind of dreadful symbol to her. Because that was what she would have had to do—plan carefully to find Mrs. Li alone and strangle her. And why the stabbing afterward? It seemed to have been a symbolic stabbing after she was dead. But no one in Ching Mei's past had been stabbed; no symbolic retribution would have required Mrs. Li's stabbing. Janet closed her eyes for a moment, closing out the picture, rejecting the possibility.

Ching Mei had been in the gathering of students Thursday evening. Could she have killed a woman and then gone to dinner with her friends? And strolled over afterward to practice English? She couldn't be such a monster!

Zhu Mei and Dawang were like other students she had met in China—friendly, interested, unencumbered by thoughts of murder or politics or past suffering. Their families were peasants, but prosperous ones. They had felt little of the upheavals in the past. The girls were loved and loving, ambitious for themselves and committed to the future of their country.

Zhu Mei seemed a little more mature than the others. She was introspective, insightful, and sensitive. She would have done well in psychology but she was heading for a career in electronics because not much was being done in the behavioral sciences in China. Janet remembered how earnestly she had told her about her ambitions. "Under Chairman Mao all of us were told to work in countryside. I learned to play violet for my future. I do not like work countryside. Can get out—in army maybe—if play violet."

"Playing the violin is good for getting into the army?" Janet was incredulous.

"If two people want go in army. One play violet . . . violin . . . one not. Play violin, get in."

"Why?"

"If unit have dance group, need play violin. I work very hard, learn play one year. Now, go to college, I do not play more."

Janet often told them about the United States, how young people were relatively free to choose their professions. Was this what the cadres would call corruption—causing rebellion among the youth? But she also told them how difficult it was for many young people to go to college, how they had to struggle to get money for tuition. The Chinese students needed only to work hard at their studies, without worrying about tuition. Of course, there were not enough colleges for all who were capable of succeeding. They didn't need her to tell them that.

Characteristically, the sensitive Zhu Mei noticed that she was dressed to go out. "Oh, you are busy. We come at wrong time."

"No, no. I was just going for a walk. But now that you're here, maybe you can help me." They probably knew the student who had run in panic from Sally's room. Maybe they also knew where he had disappeared to. "I have a question to ask you. Do any of you know Shen Luo?"

Zhu Mei wrinkled her nose. "Yes, we know him. We have classes together."

"Do you know where I can find him?"

"He is gone—to his home, I think. We do not know."

"You mean he just left—in the middle of the term?"

They shrugged, not very interested in Shen Luo.

"If you see him—if he comes back—will you tell me?" She doubted that anyone in the area would be seeing him soon. He was one of life's runners. Probably took off right from Sally's bed and never looked back. She couldn't see him stopping to murder anyone.

"Now I need a translator. Who will come with me?"

They were all enthusiastic about helping her, and followed her out to the doorman's cubicle, where Chang was reclining on the well-used bed. When he saw them, he came to the glass, nodding and smiling. The old man didn't move from the hard wooden chair —just peered at them suspiciously.

"Ask him to come out for a minute. Tell him we'd like to talk to him."

He came quickly, glad of the attention. Out of earshot of the old man, she commiserated with him over the death of the cadre, knowing he wouldn't mind that she was a little late with her sympathy. "I know that everyone here was her good friend."

He grinned widely, agreeing.

"The cook too. He was her good friend."

He nodded.

"She thought he was a very fine cook," Janet said tentatively.

"Not fine." He shook his head emphatically. "She often yelled at him because the meals for the foreigners were bad."

"She wanted a different cook?"

"No, no. She would not disgrace him. They were friends for many years. He knew her well." A sly look came over his face, like a caricature of a child putting something over on an adult. She waited. She thought he could not resist saying more. She was right. "Comrade Li is afraid of cook. He is bad, very bad."

"Chang, do you think the cook killed Mrs. Li?"

He grinned again and stopped just short of saying yes, although he embroidered on the cook's badness, hinting at his dealings with the African students, the quality of the food he bought, and, again, that Mrs. Li feared him. There was nothing really definite he could —or would—tell her.

"You know Mr. Guo, don't you, Chang?"

Yes, he knew him.

"Was he here on the day Mrs. Li was killed?"

He hadn't seen Guo. Only Mrs. Li's husband, the professor. Janet tried not to look the way she felt when she heard that.

"What time was the professor here?"

"Before dinner."

"Did you see him with Mrs. Li?"

"Yes, they were together."

"Where did you see them?"

He gestured vaguely around him. Had he really seen them on Thursday? She tried to pin him down but got the feeling that he might have been remembering other evenings, other times when Jiao Zhong En had visited his wife here.

Although she realized that Chang was probably not as out of it as everyone seemed to think, the interview left her dissatisfied and uneasy.

XING QI YI—MONDAY

1

For a while the next morning she forgot all about murder and suspects and just enjoyed teaching. These students were fun to work with—attentive, responsive, enthusiastic. If anything, they worked much too hard, spending all day and most of the night studying English. There must be a point beyond which their increasing fatigue would make the time spent a waste, but nothing could convince them of that. They were too anxious about passing the national examination, so that they would be permitted to go abroad for advanced study and research. Their children were growing up without them, their wives—or husbands—were alone, they were often lonely and even depressed. But they knew that this experience was a passport to a better life in China, aside from the fact that they could bring back new ideas to build their country's technology and economy. If some were succumbing to the "corrosive influence of bourgeois ideas" and not accepting "correct guidance"—or even being tempted to remain in the West—they were only a very small minority.

She wished all of them could pass the test but she—and they—knew that only a few would get the chance to go abroad. The others would go back to their old jobs as engineers and college teachers.

She began the class by talking for a few minutes about humor in different countries. "What people laugh about gives clues to their culture, to their values. If you can understand the jokes in a country you can understand a lot about the people."

"Do you understand Chinese jokes?"

"I've listened to the cross-talk of the Chinese comedians. The audience laughs, but when someone translates for me I don't find it so funny. I think, to appreciate the humor, you must really know the language."

"Tell us an American joke and see if we laugh."

"All right." There were many mother-in-law jokes in China, but it was mothers-in-law who told them and the focus of the humor was somewhat different. "Here's one," she said.

When she had finished there was silence, some smiles. Then Mr. Pan laughed. "It is about a mother-in-law. That is the mother of my wife. In America a man does not like the mother of his wife?"

"Well, it's not that, exactly. Many men like their mothers-in-law well enough. It's just that jokes are told about mothers-in-law. Part of the joke is pretending that all mothers-in-law are not liked."

"In China too, the wife's mother can spoil a marriage," said Wu Pin He. "My friend's wife left him because of her mother."

"They tell the daughter that the husband must do this and that. The daughter is unhappy."

"My mother-in-law is very good. She cares for the children while my wife works."

"My mother-in-law cooks for us. It is better than the dining room."

They laughed. Anything was better than the dining room.

Mr. Guo wasn't laughing. When he started to speak everyone became very quiet. "We respect the mother of my wife. He is strong woman. A soldier of the revolution."

"Oh, forgive us, Mr. Guo, Yue Zhen. It was thoughtless of me to talk about this today."

He wasn't listening. He spoke almost automatically, as if he had been thinking the words for a while. "The mother of my wife told us what was right to do. We honor him . . . her. We do what he says is right. For China. For my country."

Yue Zhen sat looking at her husband. Her face was expressionless and her hands lay quietly in her lap, palms up. She said nothing.

"We are very sorry about Mrs. Li," said Mr. Pan. But when he glanced at Janet she knew he was remembering how they had joked about force-feeding her with some of those dining-room meals as they had seen the force-feeding of the ducks on their visit to a farm commune.

*   *   *

Before the period was over Janet got an idea of what the students feared from a prolonged investigation of the murder. The door was unceremoniously flung open and three soldiers walked in. One of them began to address the class. The monitor responded, then explained: "He wishes to question us—Mr. Xu, Mr. Pan, others perhaps."

"Well," she said ungraciously, "I can't stop them."

How quickly one learns to give in to the prevailing pressures. It was not very long ago that she had firmly ushered a campus security guard out of her classroom at home. He had come in to remove a student who had been accused of hitting a teacher. "Wait," she had told him, "until the class is over." After all, the student had only been accused, not found guilty.

Now she felt helpless to prevent the interruption. Maybe it was only her inability to communicate directly with them. She noticed that they asked the questions of those who sometimes came to the Foreign Students Building. That old man at the door must keep a record.

But there was no new information for the soldiers. Yes, they sometimes came to speak English with the professor. They came also to ask questions about the lessons and to get information about American universities to which they might apply. Yes, they had all known Mrs. Li; they knew that she had not treated the professor with courtesy. The professor was very good to them; she worked hard to teach them. No, they knew nothing about Mrs. Li's death.

The questions were general, superficial, and useless. She hoped they were not going to do this very often. If they did, if it went on long enough, the students were right: they would not be prepared to take the final examination.

No one mentioned that she had been asked to play a part in the investigation. She supposed they had gone through channels and that the information had not yet filtered down to the rank and file.

She was glad when the session was over. First her insensitive mother-in-law jokes and then the interruption of the soldiers. She was tired. When she looked up from the students crowding around for a last word, she saw Mrs. Hua. She excused herself and went over to her, both of them nodding to Yue Zhen as she went out.

"Yue Zhen is a good daughter," she said. "She respects the wishes of her mother."

"Yes, she told me it was her mother's idea that she be sterilized."

"The policy of China is one child in a family. She does what must be done."

"She's not happy about it."

"Her mother tells her it is necessary. She obeys."

"What about her husband? How did he feel about it?"

"He always does what is good for China. He was a son to Mrs. Li."

"They both look so sad all the time. I don't remember when I've seen either one of them smile."

"They are very serious. Not like so many young people today who want only to enjoy themselves. They do not know how much suffering there was before the liberation. They are impatient that they do not have more material things."

"What if something happens to their child? It would be terrible for them never to be able to have another child." Janet was not interested in pursuing universal complaints against youth.

"China has too many people. We must all make sacrifices."

How fortunate for Mrs. Hua, Janet thought, that she had had her two sons before the country had made its bid for population control. How easily, and with what touching sympathy, the old were able to accept the sacrifices of the young.

2

She sat in the sunshine on a low stool and watched the little man painstakingly cut lifts for her shoes out of a slab of rubber. His was one of a number of small businesses in the shopping mall, ancient ancestor of the grand steel and glass-enclosed malls she had left behind. Actually, it was a row of connecting shacks catering to some of the everyday needs of the people in the college compound and the other residents of the area. They were all government-owned and they sold writing paper, soap, toothbrushes, and other items in one, groceries in another. (Salt was scooped into paper packets. On damp days it clumped.) There was a meat store that also sold fish when it was available, and a fruit-and-vegetable store. A branch of the post office and a bank both operated by candlelight to avoid confusion when the electricity in the city went off, as it did periodi-cally. It had taken Janet some time to realize that that was why her electric clock ran so slow: the electricity kept going off during the day while she was at work.

Outside the stores, on the unpaved lot, peasants sat before small piles of produce that they were permitted to grow and sell for themselves after they had given the state its allotment. Some were selling eggs and sunflower seeds. One was selling cabbage off the back of a truck, probably on behalf of his unit, since individuals did not own automobiles or trucks.

Other peasants had different kinds of small businesses going in the open air: shoe repairing, bicycle repairing, even pallet making under a small open-fronted tent. All day long one could hear the Jew's-harp sound of the metal slat that was used to beat the cotton batting and fluff it up. Only peasants could make money in their spare time. Workers and teachers were not permitted to moonlight.

In the middle of the lot was a great hole into which the vegetable vendors threw the vegetables that were beyond redemption. No one seemed to know if the hole had been dug for this purpose. During rainy weather, customers tracked mud into the shops and back to their rooms.

Each time Janet came up to a counter all other transactions ceased. The customers and all the salespeople crowded around waiting for her to say something. Mr. Xu had told her once that they were interested to see what foreigners bought. She laughed at that; there was not so much variety that her purchases would be different from theirs.

And here he came with his younger daughter, shopping for the family dinner—a daily chore in a country where few had refrigera-tors.

"Professor Aldane. It is good to see you," Mr. Xu greeted her. He pushed the little girl forward. "Say hello to Professor Aldane."

"Hello," she said shyly.

Janet knew that her English was very good. She had been studying it in school and with her father almost from the time she had first learned to speak. "Hello, Li Hua. How are you today?"

"I am fine today," she answered, and backed to stand behind her father.

The cobbler handed Janet her shoes. "How much?" she asked in Chinese.

It was one *kwai,* the equivalent of fifty cents for half an hour's work. She smiled, thanked him, and said goodbye: practically her whole vocabulary.

"You will buy things?" Xu asked her.

"Yes, I need some white thread. And I'd like to see if there is fruit today. I miss that in the dining room."

"The fruit is not good today. I will help you buy things."

"Oh, that's all right, Mr. Xu. I've learned how to say *zheige* and *neige* and *Duo shao qian?*—'this' and 'that' and 'How much?' "

He laughed. "You speak Chinese very well."

"Oh, sure."

He followed her into the general store anyhow, insisted on telling the clerk what she wanted, and then took the bills from her wallet when she opened it.

"I met your friend Jiao Zhong En," she told him.

"He told me so. He came to my house yesterday."

"That was a funny marriage, wasn't it?"

"Funny? I do not understand."

"Well, he doesn't seem like the kind of man who would marry Mrs. Li. He's so different from her—a teacher, a scholar."

"Yes, you are right. He was wrong to marry her. He thought it would be good. She talked to him for a very long time, to make him marry her."

"Why did he think it would be good?"

"He was very . . . uh . . . He did not do anything for years. Just study his few books. No work. No friends. His life nothing. I know this but I am in countryside. When Mrs. Li comes to university, she puts *das bao* to other teachers. She sees him. She talks to him. She does not put posters to him."

They were quiet for a while, walking slowly through the entrance to the compound.

"He says he was at your house Thursday, and that he left when you came to practice English."

"Yes. I saw him go down the path to the gate."

"Then he came back." They had almost forgotten about the little girl, but apparently she had been following the conversation.

"You saw him come back, Li Hua?"

"Oh no, she did not see him. She was doing her schoolwork."

"I saw him when my father went out. I looked from the window. He walked where they are building."

"Are you sure, Li Hua?"

"Yes. I saw him."

"Could you see what he did there?"

"No. I could only see him go behind the building where the foreigners live. I cannot see there."

"Did you see him again? Did he walk again to the gate?"

"I did not see him. My mother told me to do my work."

"Did you see anyone else walk back there where they're building?"

"Tong Ching Mei."

"Did she go there before or after Professor Jiao?"

"First she goes, then Professor Jiao."

"Did you see her come out?"

"No."

Such a serious little girl.

"I didn't realize your window faced the side of the Foreign Students Building," Janet told Xu.

"Yes. We can also see the front of the building. That is why I know when the young students come to practice their English, and I come too."

"But you can't see the back of the building, where all the building materials are?"

"No. The side of the building is too long to see the back from my window."

She would have liked to ask him if she could come to his apartment and look out of the window, to see for herself the lay of the land. But he had said several times that he would invite her to his home if it was not such a poor place, and she didn't want to embarrass him.

"Did you ever see Mrs. Li walk back there?"

"Yes. She goes to look at the work. She complains to the construction cadre that the workers do not work enough."

No, Janet thought, I will *not* pursue that one. She couldn't bear the thought of adding six or seven builders to the list of suspects.

So Jiao Zhong En had not only been at the Foreign Students Building, he had walked out back. And Ching Mei too. Both of them might have seen the body and said nothing about it. Mrs. Li had been seen walking back there at five o'clock Thursday afternoon. Colette had seen the cook being sick at five-thirty, so she thought it safe to say that Mrs. Li was dead by then, whether he had killed her or just found her. Mr. Xu came out to join the students in the courtyard at six thirty-five. Li Hua had seen them go behind the building right after her father had left the house.

The rumor that she had found the body had sprung from well-fertilized ground. Everyone could have found the body!

3

Colette was waiting for her. She opened the door and motioned Janet inside, whispering excitedly even after the door was closed behind them. "I just heard something very . . ." The word eluded her. "I will tell you, that old woman has much to answer for!"

Janet grinned. "It must be dirt, you sound so happy about it."

"Dirt?" She didn't understand but she brushed the word aside. "She makes such scandal about others but she herself is not so innocent."

"Mrs. Li?"

"They respect her, yes. But when they all know they will not respect her."

"What is it?"

"Do you know—she has a child."

"Yes. Yue Zhen. Everyone knows that."

"No, not Yue Zhen. Another child. Long after she is a widow. No one knows this except the cook. He knew her then, in the country. Chang, he hears them shouting. The cook says he will tell about the child. The old woman says he must not."

That must have been the scene she witnessed in the courtyard outside her window, Janet thought. Then it was not the cook being threatened; it was Mrs. Li. Chang was right when he said she was afraid of the cook, but he hadn't mentioned the details. Talking through an interpreter was definitely not satisfactory.

"Interesting. I wonder where the child is."

Colette shrugged. What did it matter? The old woman had been vulnerable—that was the point. Who cared where the child was?

"Well, wherever the child is, I hope Mrs. Li treated her better than she did Yue Zhen," Janet said. "Would you like tea? Come to my room."

"No, no tea." And she was gone. Janet's response to the news did not show the proper degree of gloating gratification.

As she sat with her tea cooling, the faces of Yue Zhen, Mrs. Li, and Jiao Zhong En floated between her and the open newspaper in her lap. Blackmail. To someone like Mrs. Li, the secret of a child born out of wedlock would be one she would keep at all costs. Outside the building where she kept the workers comfortable, people were wary of her, respectful but keeping their distance. She must have known how quickly they would begin to whisper as she passed, to laugh behind her back, to speak in shocked voices. Her righteousness probably made them feel guilty about their own small lapses from dogma, and who knew when she would discover one of them and bring public shame. The respect they had for her would quickly dissipate in a cloud of scandal.

Had Jiao Zhong En known of the child, or had he too just discovered the secret? She could not imagine him reacting with any great show of emotion. Life had already done its worst to him, forcing him from his university, depriving him of his books, setting him to work in the fields. His air of gentle detachment was a shield protecting him from whatever new shocks assaulted those around him. Since he could do nothing to alter the course of events he would be still and let them flow around him.

4

Down the corridor she heard the voice of one of the maids, loud and giggly, talking rapidly and almost without pause. Occasionally a small murmur indicated that she was not talking to herself. It was shower time for the general public. That small murmur, to whom did it belong? Most of the women who worked in the building, and their friends who came in to use the shower, all spoke incessantly and loudly.

Yes, of course. That little country girl, Yanmin. Everyone knew she was the child of Mrs. Li's friend. The cook must have known that friend, if he knew about Mrs. Li's illegitimate child. This girl must have been born at about the same time, when the Cultural Revolution was at its height and so many city people were roaming the countryside. That must also have been about the time Mrs. Li met Jiao Zhong En. Did he know the mother of this girl?

What had he said yesterday? Something to do with the child. The child. Which child—this one, or Mrs. Li's? What was it?

5

At dinner that night the cook and his staff sat at their round table having a voluble discussion in voices they didn't bother to lower. Yanmin was dispiritedly making the rounds of the drooping plants on the windowsills, awkwardly pouring water into each from a porcelain basin. Occasionally she would turn her head toward the others, listen for a moment to what they were saying, and then turn back to her task. She looked very unhappy, on the verge of tears.

When she had finished the plants, she put the basin down on an unoccupied table, where it would remain until the next regional meeting required the use of the table for eating. A man came into the dining room. He looked tired and dirty, as if he had traveled a long way. He removed his tunic and, in his undershirt, began to wash himself thoroughly in the sink at the side of the room. The seven foreigners, sitting huddled together at one table poking at plates of food, never raised an eyebrow. Depression seemed to have descended on everyone, as if to each the enormity of the act called murder was finally real.

Suddenly there was an altercation among the dining-room workers. Yanmin, who had wandered over to join them, began to shout. Her anger was directed against the cook, who sprang to his feet and shouted back at her. The wet cigarette fell from his mouth. He waved his arms and his face swelled until his eyes disappeared, making him look like a very angry pig. Yanmin, reduced to tears, stood there sobbing, unable to shout anymore, or even to speak.

"What was that all about?" Janet asked.

Sally shook her head. Her Chinese wasn't good enough to get even one word of that kind of argument.

"That is a great surprise," said Colette.

"The old woman has one friend to speak for her," laughed Masomakali.

Ka Ka Chi said thoughtfully, "Someone mourns for her. It is very bad to have no one to cry when a person dies."

"What did she say to them? Why was she so angry?"

"It was the cook she was angry with. He was telling all the terrible things Mrs. Li did to everyone." When he had stayed home for several days, too sick to come to work, she had reported him for malingering and he had been publicly reprimanded by the committee. She had refused permission for the young helper to go to school; he wanted to work as a tourist guide and he knew he would have a chance at that if he learned English. She had told the cadre in charge of transfers that he was good only for working in a dining room. She had told the unit to reduce the allocation for food, implying that too much of the money was going to feed the cook and his helpers.

Masomakali called to Yanmin and she came tearfully to their table. He said something to her and she answered him. "The girl says it is all lies. She says Mrs. Li was a very good woman."

"Did everybody who worked in the building like her?" Janet asked.

"She says yes, everybody. She is good to workers."

"Who would want to kill her? If everybody loved her, who killed her?"

"Bad man. Thief maybe." She began to sob, the only sign of sorrow Janet had seen since the discovery of the murder.

"Ask her if she knew Mrs. Li before she came to work here."

Yanmin spoke at great length. As she recalled Mrs. Li's kindness her sobbing ceased.

"Yes, she knows her since she is little girl. Mrs. Li was friend of her mother. Her family are peasants. Mrs. Li brings her to Beijing from countryside to work here."

"What else did Mrs. Li do for her?"

"She sends her to primary school. She buys her pretty things."

Janet looked at the regulation blue cotton pants and white blouse. What pretty things, for heaven's sake?

The girl darted out of the dining room and returned in a moment, carefully unwinding a strip of knitted cloth from a small china figurine. Janet had seen thousands of them in the stores, cheap, assembly-line figures, indifferently molded and painted. This one was of Guan Yin, an ancient princess who, if she remembered correctly, had been good to the poor and had died for love. Yanmin held it tenderly for a moment, then slowly wrapped it up again. As she did so, she began to cry, this time softly, the tears running down her cheeks and dripping on the gift she cherished.

Such tenderness for the child of a friend, thought Janet. And for her own daughter, nothing but unsympathetic, even unfeeling, stoicism.

6

Lying in bed, Janet finally closed her book. There was something bothering her, something she was forgetting kept interfering with her concentration. Was it something she had seen or heard? She knew that if she remembered it she would have the key to a part of the puzzle of Mrs. Li. As she drifted off to sleep she thought she almost had it, but then it was gone again.

She went flying down the stairs, leaping a whole flight at a time. What freedom! What joy! To fly like this and land at the foot of each flight as lightly as a dandelion clock! Jiao Zhong En stood smiling up at her from the bottom of each flight, his arms outstretched ready to catch her. But she didn't need his help. Each time her toes touched the landing like feathers, and then she was flying again.

Yue Zhen caught her ankle as she flew and held it tightly. She struggled to release herself, and when she looked again it wasn't Yue Zhen but Yanmin. She kept struggling to free herself and sat up to find her foot stuck in a gap in the stitching that held the cotton cover on the brocade quilt. She heard herself say, "Mrs. Li treated Yanmin like a daughter."

She sank back on the pillow. The face of Jiao Zhong En floated before her half-closed eyes. She found it easier to think of him as Jiao than Zhong En. The name was awkward on her tongue. Zhong En. Zhong En. She would learn to say it, she knew. Saying it would conjure up his face in her mind, as it did now. She was becoming very fond of him. One day the suspicions would all be gone.

At three in the morning she opened her eyes again and said calmly, "Of course." Jiao Zhong En knew about the child. He had told her so. He had said some women did not have enough love for all their children. They gave what love they had to only one and the others went begging. *But it was a tragedy for the one who was loved because that one's life was never her own.* He had said that as if he was talking about someone he knew very well. And he had said "her own," not the generic "one's own." They had just seen Yanmin pass and his eyes had followed her as he talked.

That girl is Mrs. Li's daughter, Janet thought, and her husband knows it!

Her heart lurched at the realization. The question forced its way back into her mind, and she argued with it: even if he had just found out about the illegitimate child, why should he care what had happened before their marriage to a woman he hadn't liked much anyhow? The Chinese might be hung up about sex but no man would kill his wife because of a child born eighteen years ago, before she had married him.

XING QI ER—TUESDAY

1

When she came out of the classroom building at noon the next day Jiao Zhong En was waiting for her. She thought about him so much that their friendship seemed to her almost to be rooted in a past they had shared. She wondered if he felt the same.

As they walked back to her room together he told her that he had been summoned by the police again. It was more convenient for them to do their questioning at the Foreign Students Building.

"You must be worn out with all this."

"It is difficult, yes. To hear how people felt about her. Although one knows these things, to hear them again and again . . ."

"Your wife was very good to take her friend's child and care for her." Janet felt a pang of guilt. Was she trying to comfort him or pump him?

"Yes," he said bitterly. "Very good. She brought her here and put her to work in the dining room. Without education, she will be there her whole life. She will marry another like her. Her life is ruined."

She was surprised at his vehemence. He had talked about Yue Zhen's lack of education so matter-of-factly: "She followed the precepts of Mao to see the country, to learn from the peasants. And her mother encouraged her. She gave up the opportunity for education; now it is too late for her." He hadn't seemed disturbed about that, seemed hardly to care that Yue Zhen now had periodic urges to learn English so she could improve her position. As far as Janet knew, he never offered to help his stepdaughter.

Surely all this bitterness was not about a stranger's child. He must be the father of Yanmin. Why else would he feel so strongly about her? Had he always known about his child or had he just found out?

Her perception of Jiao Zhong En was changing rapidly. Her initial attraction to a handsome, erudite, and quiet man was not lessened by her growing awareness of the complexity of the man, the secrets he covered with his quiet manner, the storms that raged inside him.

"Did I understand correctly the other day? You've never had a child?"

His face became a rigid mask. His silence was all the answer she needed. "I did not tell you what was not true," he finally said.

"No," she said gently. "I know. I misunderstood." You wanted me to misunderstand, so I did, she added to herself.

He nodded. "So many years I did not know." His voice was low. "So many years she kept my child from me."

"How did you find out?"

"Yue Zhen told me. She heard talk here. People knew."

"People knew Yanmin is your daughter?"

"No, they knew she was my wife's daughter. When I learned of this I asked my wife. She told me the girl was our child, a child she had after I had been forced to run from Qinghai Province. She did not know where I had gone. When she was able to find me again, the child had already been born in an isolated farmhouse. Everyone thought it was her friend's child. She never told me. I wanted to kill her. For the first time in my life I could have killed."

Janet looked nervously over her shoulder. "Don't say things like that."

"It does not matter. She should have told me. Even if she told no one else she should have told me."

"What will you do now?"

He didn't answer. She thought he hadn't heard her.

"Zhong En?"

"Now?" he said vaguely.

"Will you tell Yanmin that you are her father?"

He looked at her as if he didn't understand what she was saying. "Tell? No. How can I tell? She kept the secret for so many years. I cannot tell." He put his hand to his eyes.

He may be hating his wife, she thought as she watched his despair, but it doesn't look as if he's going to do anything different from what she did. This gentle detachment might be an overrated commodity.

2

At lunch, Haji, Masomakali, Ka Ka Chi, Colette, Sally, and Janet sat together. Their eyes kept moving to the other table, where Jiao Zhong En, the cook, and the two policemen sat speaking in low voices. They might have been having a serious group discussion about a subject that was of great interest to all four of them. Occasionally they would pause and sit without speaking, deep in thought, more like old friends than policemen and suspects.

The cook called to bring tea and Yanmin brought it. The officer said something to her and she remained standing at the table while the talk went on. Finally Jiao motioned to her and she sat down on one of the empty chairs, saying nothing, just listening to the men talking and looking very sad.

When the officer got up and approached the table of foreigners, only Janet smiled and said hello. Masomakali stared at his plate. Colette looked frightened. He nodded in response to Janet's greeting, said something, and motioned her to the other table. Jiao rose when she came up and gave her a small smile. The officer pointed to an empty chair.

There was silence for a moment, then he asked a question. "He asks if you think about the people who were here Thursday night."

"Think about them?"

"Yes. He says that you know about these things. You work with the police in your country. Now you will work with him. He believes you have . . . uh . . . insight. He thinks that when you look at people, when you talk to them, you understand much. I think so too."

"Don't expect too much," she hedged.

"He asks first what you think of the cook."

The fat man kept his eyes on her while she spoke, nothing in his face or piggy eyes revealing any emotion. For once the dirty cigarette was missing from the corner of his mouth.

And in the end it was not her "insight" she shared with them; it was what she was remembering. "The last time I saw him on Thursday night was at dinner. When we left the dining room he was sitting at one of the round tables with the other workers. But he wasn't eating. That was unusual."

She tried to remember if he looked sick or upset but she wasn't sure if knowing he had been vomiting a short time earlier would influence her memory. She said nothing about it, except to repeat significantly, "He always ate with the others and he ate a great deal. But not that night."

"You did not see him leave the building?"

"No." She thought a moment. "That's odd. Now that I think of it, he usually leaves while I'm sitting outside with the students. The bench I sit on faces the entrance and I can see him leave. I didn't see him that night."

"Perhaps you have just forgotten."

"Perhaps. You might check with some of the others. They may remember, because every time I saw him leave I said something uncomplimentary about him and everybody laughed."

There was something uncomfortable in the laughter, she knew. Was it because a foreigner was criticizing one of their own and there was some resentment even though they knew he deserved the criticism? Or were they uncomfortably aware that the cook was a man of influence? There was, perhaps, always the fear that one of the group might report the laugh to a cadre.

The cook's eyes never wavered. But then, her opinion of him could not have come as a surprise. And the food couldn't get any worse—could it?

"What about the cook's helpers, all those who worked in the dining room?"

"They all left together on Thursday. But before that—was it Tuesday or Wednesday?—I saw the two young men and the woman who serves the food leaving. She was putting on her jacket as they came out. I remember they waved good night to me."

She looked at Yanmin. "They stopped and called back inside to Yanmin. They had to wait a couple of minutes before she came out. She was putting her jacket on too." Her eyes remained on Yanmin, who shifted in her chair and frowned. "She looked different. She was always so calm, so contented, moving from one thing to another so quietly, as if nothing in the world could bother her. But that night she . . ." Her voice faded as she recalled the scene.

Then she spoke again slowly. "She seemed confused. Yes, that was it—confused. She was struggling to get her arm in the sleeve of her jacket as she hurried out. Then she stopped and looked back inside, maybe at someone I couldn't see. And she stood there with her arm back and the sleeve dangling, as if she had forgotten that she hadn't finished putting on the jacket. Then the four of them went out through the gate. They were talking to her. Her sleeve was still dangling."

When Jiao Zhong En translated what she said, Yanmin started to get up, but a word from the officer made her sit again. She began to cry. Jiao spoke softly to her and she looked up at him gratefully. The officer asked her something and she shook her head. He asked again, insistently. Jiao also urged her. When she answered tearfully, the cook grunted, and the officer's aide motioned him to be silent. The girl continued to speak.

When she finished, everyone turned to the cook. His face seemed to have puffed up until his eyes were almost hidden. They waited but he said nothing, and an element of menace entered the silence. Finally he blurted out a staccato sentence. It sounded poisonous, vindictive, and the girl gasped. Jiao's face became a blank.

The officer rapped out a command and the cook spoke again. Janet couldn't restrain herself. "What is it?"

The officer looked at the cook speculatively for some time. The fat man, his head lowered, stared back with a belligerence that slowly faded. Jiao explained: As Yanmin was leaving that night the cook had made some comment about the old woman being too much trouble, always running around disturbing things and threatening people. Yanmin had objected, saying he had no right to talk about a good woman and a respected cadre that way. She said he hated Mrs.

Li because she was so honest, so upright, always doing what was good for the country.

Then the cook had muttered that it was not surprising that she felt the way she did. The old woman was, after all, her own flesh and blood. She had thought at first that she hadn't heard him correctly, but he had repeated it. And then had refused to say any more and told her to go home—to get out.

Now the cook revealed what he meant by what he had said. He had information that Mrs. Li was Yanmin's mother, not the friend of her mother as everyone had thought. He knew the friend—had known both her and Mrs. Li many years ago when they had all been in the country. It had not been much of a secret then, although Mrs. Li thought she was fooling everyone. She had spent some time in another village. She had been more important than most of them, he sneered. She had traveled on government business. When she returned, people had begun to whisper. Then she and her friend had gone away again. The friend's husband had just been killed in some fighting between the villagers and a band of youths who had passed through the town.

When the two women returned there was a baby. They had said the baby had been born to the new widow. But the whispers had gone on for a long time. Everyone knew the truth.

"But how can he be sure that Mrs. Li really was Yanmin's mother?"

"He says the birth was registered correctly. The midwife and some of the other women in the place where the baby was born knew. My wife was known to them, so they could not register a false name. The cook learned this from the friend. He says the friend hated my wife too. She loved the baby and she hated . . ." Jiao's voice faltered.

Janet felt guilty. People kept forgetting that he was the husband of the murdered woman. She wondered why the officer didn't ask him if he had known about all this, but he merely told the girl she could leave. Jiao managed to pat her hand as she went back to the kitchen.

A secret kept for eighteen years, and the cook had betrayed it in a moment. This could have been the last straw for Mrs. Li. She had objected to his incompetence and thievery but she continued to permit it as long as he kept her secret. But now that Yanmin knew, had Mrs. Li given the cook an ultimatum? And had he, in a spasm of anger and fear, strangled her?

3

The officer spoke again, and she heard the name Ka Ka Chi.

"He asks can you tell something about the Africans. His experience with these foreigners is very small. Perhaps the one called Ka Ka Chi."

"Ka Ka Chi never says much. Thursday he finished dinner before I did and left the table to go outside. When I came out he was sitting on the step in front of the door. Then Masomakali came out and sat with him. Haji had left the table without eating. He does that often. He says the food is for animals, not people. I don't know where he went between the time he left the table and when he came out to join Ka Ka Chi and Masomakali."

"How did he look when he came out?"

"Not as furious as he usually does. He always has such an angry face. This time he looked calm. He even smiled when he talked to Ka Ka Chi."

The officer said something to his aide, who then went to the other table and brought Ka Ka Chi and Haji back. They were told to sit.

"You spoke to Mrs. Li on Thursday evening, after you left the dining room?" the officer asked Haji.

The young man looked startled and started to protest. "Why do you say I saw the old woman? I did not . . ."

"Do not bother to deny it." The tone was steely. He would give no quarter to *this* suspect. She thought perhaps it was because he shared the prevailing opinion of Africans. Up until only the year before, screens had separated the African students from the Europeans and Americans in the dining room. All the foreigners had finally united to demand their removal. "What did you speak about?"

"It is not true! Who said I spoke to her?"

"You were seen."

Janet's eyebrows rose when Jiao translated this. It sounded like an old B movie.

"No! I spoke to her on Wednesday. I did not see her on Thursday."

"What did you speak about?" He would take anything he could get. Wednesday's conversation was better than nothing.

"I did not kill her."

"What did you talk about?"

"What else? She was cheating us. She and this pig of a cook. What did I have to speak to her about? I wanted only something to eat like a person, not an animal. I told her I could stand it no longer."

"And what would you do? You would kill her for this?"

"No, no. One does not kill, even though one is brought to the limits of one's endurance. These people are . . . !" He ended his outburst in Swahili. He had reached the limits, not only of his endurance but of his ability to express himself in Chinese. Nobody asked him to translate. The meaning was clear.

Then he began to bluster. "I will not be questioned in this way! I will report this to my embassy! I am here as a guest of the government and I will be treated with respect!"

The officer seemed bored and waved him away. He did not want to listen to this. Haji stalked out of the room.

"That one does not associate much with the people here," the officer commented.

"Haji. There is one angry young man."

"Yes, the one who throws his meals at the cook."

She laughed. "Not exactly at the cook. Just on the floor. An appropriate place for that food. If the cook had been strangled I think I'd say Haji had done it."

He turned to Ka Ka Chi and asked if he had seen Mrs. Li on Thursday evening.

"I saw her before dinner, in the office. I went in to buy food tickets. I greeted her, that is all."

"She was alone?"

"No. The two women were there, the one who gives the tickets and the one who takes the money. They are always there."

"Did you leave Mrs. Li in the office?"

"Yes. I went to the dining room. She remained there. I did not see her again."

"Did you also have arguments with her?"

"No. I do not argue. I wait my time. I study. I leave China. It will be soon."

Janet nodded when Jiao translated. Yes, that was what he was like: quiet, stoic, biding his time. If things were bad for him, no one would know it. But she wondered if one day, as a leader in his own country, he would demand his due for the years of his youth he had spent as an alien in a hostile land.

When Ka Ka Chi had left the dining room, the officer sent the cook and Yanmin back to the kitchen. "The other African," he asked, "the tall one. Do you think he could kill?"

"Masomakali?"

"Perhaps he hears Mrs. Li threaten the cook. He fears to lose his . . . er . . ." Zhong En stumbled for the word. "Supplier?" Janet asked.

"Yes. He asks if you believe he could kill when under the influence of drugs."

She looked at the officer, astonished. "He knows about the drugs?"

The officer spoke at some length: "We are not so different from your own police. We often know that such things exist but we are unable to find the individuals who are responsible and the material evidence. We wait, we search, we sometimes find one or two such criminals and we stop them. But the problem is a complex one. Essentially, I think, we cannot solve the problem because we cannot solve the problem of individual greed."

"Even in a socialist society?" she teased Jiao.

"Even in a socialist society." He looked grave but his eyes held a smile.

"I don't think Masomakali would stab someone after she was dead. Under the influence of drugs, in the grip of a momentary craziness, he might hurt someone—maybe even strangle a person. But then to take a knife and deliberately . . ." She shuddered. "No. I can't see him doing that."

"There is a kind of strength in that. He is not a strong man." The officer had observed these foreigners more closely than he admitted.

"You mean strength of purpose? Yes. Someone made a calculated decision—a deliberate point. It was done coolly, because it had to be done. There would be nothing cool about a killing done by Maso-makali. Any action he took would be in the heat of passion."

"Ka Ka Chi, on the other hand, is not at all passionate. A very quiet man."

"He's also a sensitive man. Masomakali is his friend and he cares for him. I've seen Ka Ka Chi trying to convince him to eat when he's on such a high that he won't think of food or sleep."

"High?"

"Yes. When the drugs make him feel unrealistically happy, opti-mistic, joyous, so that he doesn't think of realities, like food."

"Could Ka Ka Chi have killed for a friend—a friend who was threatened with being sent home?"

"Was he ever threatened with that?"

He shook his head. "We have not heard of this. But if his school-work was not being done . . ."

"He wasn't having trouble in class. His drug taking seems to be restricted to weekends, and only occasionally on a day when he's feeling particularly lonely and unhappy. At any rate, I doubt that your government would be so quick to deport one of these young Africans. It might cause political repercussions that neither China nor any of the African countries would want to confront at this time."

He didn't answer, as if he was reluctant to discuss any aspect of international politics with a foreigner.

"You are so certain that one of the Africans is not responsible?" There was skepticism in the question.

"Don't tell me you're one of those who believe that Africans are not civilized!"

"No, I do not share that view held by so many of my countrymen. I only think that they are young and strong and very angry. They have been angry for a long time and it is not the kind of anger that grows less at their age."

Janet shrugged. If he thought she was so insightful, how come he wasn't quicker to accept her assessment of these young men? A prophet is without honor everywhere.

She grinned at herself and stretched. The PLA men seemed ready to end this session.

4

The soldiers left the compound shortly after that, taking Zhong En with them. After dinner they were back again, sitting at one of the dining-room tables with some of the workers.

When Janet left the building, Zhong En caught up and walked along with her. "Where are you going?" he asked.

"To see a movie. Would you like to come too?"

"Yes," he said. "The soldiers are finished with me." He sighed and added, "There is nothing more I can tell them."

"Come along," she said cheerfully. "It will do us both good."

She looked back and saw all the others trailing behind—Sally, Ka Ka Chi, Masomakali, even Haji. Only Colette was missing. Everyone went when there was a movie. Today it had been announced that the simultaneous translation would be in English. They took turns with English and French, the only two languages still being taught in the college. The few earphones were reserved for the foreigners on campus.

Near the auditorium Zhong En stopped to greet a young man who was walking in the opposite direction. He wouldn't look at her when Zhong En introduced him as Liu, but mumbled something and walked quickly on. They continued toward the entrance, shuffling forward as the bottleneck at the door moved slowly. Suddenly Janet was saying, "Save me a seat, Zhong En. I'll be back." And she turned back the way they had come.

At the other end of the compound, she skirted the Foreign Students Building and stepped off the path into sand. She thought she saw a shadow disappear through the entrance of the new building and she hurried to catch up. At the foot of the stairs she called up to him. "Liu. Please stop. I'd like to talk to you."

There was only silence. She couldn't even hear feet continuing to ascend the concrete stairs.

"Please don't be afraid. I don't think you're doing anything wrong. I just want to ask a question."

Nothing.

"Liu, do you want to see a murderer go free? You're Zhong En's friend. It was his wife who was murdered."

For a long moment, only silence. Then, from up the stairwell, a low voice. "I cannot say. There are others here."

"I won't tell anyone about you. I promise."

He was there beside her. She had not heard him make his way down. She swallowed hard. "Colette says she saw the cook through the window. Did you see him too?"

"Why do you think so? We told you we do not go into the rooms. We remain where there are no windows."

"I think you did see something. You wouldn't have panicked when I came into the building. I could have been seriously hurt when you ran into me."

"I did not want to hurt you. I knew it was you."

"You saw the cook, didn't you?"

"Yes," he said reluctantly. "I knew you would ask that. We hear that you are asking questions about Comrade Li."

"Did the cook kill Comrade Li?"

"That I do not know. I see him with knife in hand. And then he is sick."

"You could see what he had in his hand? Wasn't it dark?"

"A light struck it from somewhere for a moment. A . . . uh . . . uh . . . sparkle? gleam?"

"Yes, I understand. That's all you saw? He didn't . . . er . . . use the knife?"

"That is all I saw."

"Could you see if there was blood on the knife?"

She thought he shook his head.

"Thank you. I appreciate your talking to me. Believe me, your secret is safe with me."

Making her way out, she wondered how she could tell the officer about this without betraying the squatters. She was sure now that the cook had murdered Mrs. Li. The evidence might not be absolutely conclusive, but how many murders had front-row witnesses? And even eyewitnesses were notoriously unreliable. This latest piece of evidence might be all the police needed to complete their case.

She found the officer and his aide still sitting at the table in the dining room. They had finished eating and were now relaxing and smoking. She started to move toward them and then remembered and looked frantically about for someone who could translate. Only a couple of dining-room workers were visible. She took a deep breath and scrabbled in her mind for words. *"Wo bidei* . . . uh . . . I must . . . er . . . I have to . . ."

She floundered. She felt shackled, her brain bound in irons. She put her hands to her head as if she felt the pain.

"You have discovered something?"

Her jaw dropped and she stared, dumbfounded. His face remained bland, but his eyes twinkled.

"Discovered?"

"Something you wish to tell me?"

"Uh . . . yes. I believe," she said without preamble, "that the cook is the murderer."

When the officer said nothing she pulled out a chair and sat, breathing deeply to calm herself. "Do you want to hear?" she finally asked.

He nodded.

"Well, we all know Mrs. Li was essentially an honest woman and a patriot. She must have hated the cook's activities. She must have told him so many times."

He nodded again.

"He probably hated her for her morality, the contempt she felt for him. But she couldn't get rid of him because he knew the secret about her child. So they continued to argue and threaten each other —but it was a stalemate. Neither could move against the other. Then, when he practically told Yanmin about her true birth, Yanmin must have dragged the rest of the story from her mother. The cook no longer had power over Mrs. Li. Her secret was out. Now she could see to it that he lost his job—maybe worse. This time the argument led to murder."

The officer flicked the ash of his cigarette on the littered table. "The logic is persuasive but it is not evidence."

"He was seen with a knife where Mrs. Li was found!" She blurted it out without volition, so eager was she to convince him.

He looked at her calmly, then slowly stood up. "We know the Frenchwoman saw the cook when he was sick. She said nothing of a knife."

"You know she was in the unfinished building?"

"Yes. We questioned one of the students living there. He told us."

"I thought no one knew—that they were doing something illegal."

He shrugged. "They do no harm. It is difficult to find a place to live."

Yes, she thought fleetingly. The everyday discretionary power is always in the hands of the police—in a democracy or socialist state. Liu and the others were probably unaware that one of their number had talked to the police. "Well, then, I can tell you. One of them saw him holding a knife before he was sick. Don't ask me which one; I couldn't identify him," she added quickly.

He turned abruptly and said something in Chinese to the other man, and they both strode from the dining room without another glance at her.

Feeling somewhat deflated, but still a little breathless, Janet went back to the auditorium and found Zhong En. They sat side by side in the dark, shoulders touching. She was more conscious of that touching than she was of the crazy translation coming through the earphones. Once, though, she couldn't help laughing. Zhong En smiled. He's really gorgeous when he smiles! The thought surprised her and she felt her face flush in the dark.

She smiled back. He leaned toward her and put his lips for a moment on hers. When the screen faded out and the auditorium lights went on, she almost thought she had imagined the kiss, but he was still looking at her, half smiling. He took her arm, reminding her that it was time to leave. She flushed again at his touch, and then told herself to grow up.

They walked slowly back toward the Foreign Students Building, where he had left his bicycle in one of the racks in the wall-less shed. They talked about the clear night, how large the moon looked. He said when all the trees in the compound began to flower in the spring it was a beautiful sight and he often came to see it. The fragrance was unbelievably sweet.

In the darkness of the shed she felt his fingers interlace with hers. "Good night," he whispered. It felt like a caress.

She watched him ride down the path and then turned and strolled to the building.

Xing Qi San—Wednesday

1

"They have come to arrest the cook!" Colette announced triumphantly at breakfast the next day. "They are searching for him everywhere but they cannot find him!"

Masomakali came bursting into the dining room, speaking wildly in French. Janet could catch nothing of what he was saying, but she thought she could guess enough. He was in a panic at the news that his connection was gone. She wondered how they treated addiction in China.

Ka Ka Chi translated. "He says that they found drugs in the cook's room. Now they will arrest him."

"Not for the murder?" Janet asked.

"Masomakali does not know. He knows only that they look for the man to arrest him."

"Has he run away?"

"He was not in his room. He did not sleep there last night."

Janet went out to see what was happening. As she opened the door, several workers came running from the back of the building, gesticulating madly, almost knocking her down and barreling into the two soldiers who were coming out of the office. Suddenly everyone was running—Colette, Sally, Ka Ka Chi, Masomakali.

"What is it?" Janet yelled at them. "What are they saying?"

"They have found the cook!" Colette yelled back, although they were not twelve inches from each other.

"What?"

"The cook! He is killed! In the back! As Mrs. Li!"

"What?"

Colette ran toward the back of the building followed by the others. The two policemen were the last on the scene.

He was lying on his side at the foot of the pile of sand, uncannily like the way Mrs. Li had lain the previous week. One of the policemen pulled at his shoulder and he rolled over on his back. His eyes were open, one eye filled with sand. There was no sign of the violence that had been done to him. He was dead—but what had killed him?

The officer moved the body to its other side, looking for some sign of the cause of death. Through a haze of nausea Janet marveled at how little concern he seemed to have for any clues and material evidence he might be disturbing. He began to talk, and Colette explained. "He was not killed."

"He's *not* dead?"

"Yes, yes," she said impatiently. "He is dead. But no person does it. He is just dying."

"Was he poisoned?"

"Poison? Why do you ask that? Do you know of poison?"

Everyone turned to listen for her answer. "Maybe he ate some of his own cooking last night, and *that* poisoned him." She giggled.

Colette looked horrified, and then began to laugh too. Sally giggled and Masomakali bellowed louder and louder, clearly out of control.

The officer looked incredulous for a moment, and then said sternly, "What are you all laughing at?"

They all stopped immediately. Fear and horror quickly extinguished any desire to laugh. The officer spoke again and Ka Ka Chi answered him.

"They will call the . . . uh . . . ambulance, I think. They must discover how he died. But the police think heart, perhaps. Not poison," he added.

Janet almost giggled again.

2

There was no reason for them all to continue standing there, but no one seemed to know how to leave. Even the two soldiers remained, murmuring to each other. But someone had apparently started the necessary routines. An olive-drab station wagon drew up in the courtyard and a man and woman dressed in army uniforms got out. The aide walked slowly to them and they stood talking—longer than seemed necessary to tell them to pick up the body and take it to the morgue.

The officer spoke to her. "They go to the hospital," he said.
"Hospital?"
"To find the cause of dying."
"Oh yes. I see."
"You will walk with me, please?"
"Yes, of course." She fell in beside him. Like a fool, she said the obvious. "You speak English very well."
"I do not speak well," he answered with customary Chinese humility. "My English is very poor."
My Chinese should be so poor, she thought.
They walked together out of the gate onto the path that cut across the compound. He held his hands clasped behind his back, like the lord of the manor. "You believe yet that the cook kills Comrade Li?"
"Why not? Isn't it the most likely answer?" To her ears she sounded defensive. Why wasn't it the cook? None of the evidence had changed, just because he had died. But she was not really satisfied that it was all over. The words *modus operandi* came to mind. Petty chiselers didn't murder people. They were liars, bullies—but they lived always looking over their shoulders, frightened little men. They would run before they would murder.
She kept trying to identify a motive that she could understand and accept wholeheartedly. The Chinese people were not really so different from Americans. If someone was murdered, it would be because of some fear, some desire, some emotion that people in her own country killed for. When she tried to communicate this to the man beside her, he had no trouble understanding her.
"I agree, I think. But the strong feelings in this matter are all old —so many people with feelings from the past."
"You think she must have been killed for something that just happened—that happened very recently?"
"Yes. Very great anger needed to . . ." He made a motion of strangling with his hands.
"And the knife too. Why that?"
He shrugged. "To be sure she is dead? Perhaps she was to be killed with knife, but anger comes too quickly. Knife is hidden, difficult to grasp."
Strangled in the heat of fury. And then rummaging for the knife under the shirt and stabbing to make sure. A shudder went through her. He noticed and shook his head in empathy.

"If that's true, then that would eliminate Xu and Ching Mei. Their sufferings were part of the Cultural Revolution and that was a long time ago."

"Yes. There was anger. Now only sadness. All is past."

"And I don't think her daughter would have done this. She did what her mother wanted her to do. Why kill her now?" Well, of course, she thought, just in sheer frustration and regret at what had been done. Knuckle under to the bully, then one day the smoldering anger erupts and a strength is called up that was never there before. It was possible.

"One is forced to do certain things. The anger comes afterward." He echoed her thought.

"Where did you study English?"

"Mostly myself. Television teaches also."

"Fantastic! There aren't many Americans who have learned a foreign language on their own that way!" She remembered how many years she had studied French in school and still could not speak it as well as this man spoke English.

He changed the subject. "Do you think of the others?"

She shook her head, reluctant to admit doubts about people she cared for. "Mostly I thought the cook. He's the one who seemed mixed up in all kinds of shady things."

"Yes, we know of his activities. Not a good . . . uh . . . citizen?" He laughed as he found the word. Citizen—*gongining*—was not used in Chinese in quite the same way.

"Maybe that's why he died; his heart couldn't stand the strain of murdering Mrs. Li."

"Yes, perhaps it is finished."

"But you don't believe it. You don't think he killed her."

He shook his head. "Comrade Li has known many years the crimes this man does. Can she now reveal? She also is guilty."

"You think she would do nothing?"

He shrugged. "They would continue the anger between them, the fighting, the threats. Perhaps one day he would be discovered—by another." Abruptly he asked, "You become friends with her husband, Jiao Zhong En?"

"He's my teacher," she said quickly—and felt herself getting warm under his thoughtful gaze.

"Yes." Noncommittal.

"He's very sad about his wife's death." Now that was a stupid thing to say! This man was no fool. Anyone could see that Zhong En wasn't exactly broken up about the loss of his wife.

"Did you know him before the murder?"

"No. I met him here the day Mrs. Li's body was discovered."

"And he became your teacher."

"Yes." She said it defiantly. "What's wrong with that?"

He looked at her quizzically. "Wrong? Is there something wrong?"

"No, of course not. He's a very good teacher."

"Yes. A scholar." A pause. "Mrs. Li was not educated."

She waited. She had said enough. This man would begin to think there *was* something wrong.

"Is your knee better?" he asked, shocking her at the connection he seemed to be making.

"How did you know about . . . ?"

"Unfinished buildings can be dangerous."

He looked at her for a moment, then pointed behind her. "Your classes are in this building?"

She nodded wordlessly and went in.

3

When she came out of her class at noon, Wang Qu Qing met her at the door. "They have not found the murderer yet. But the cook died of a bad heart," he announced.

"How do you know this?" she teased him.

"I know," he said, and smiled archly.

"Are the police still here?"

"No, they are not here. There is nothing more to know here. Perhaps they will arrest someone soon."

"And do you know whom they will arrest?"

He pondered this, shook his head, and changed the subject. "Do you go to Friendship Store today?"

"Why? Do you want me to buy something for you?"

"I would like to go with you. They are having jeans."

"What do you want with jeans?" They were, she knew, one of the banned fashions.

"Not for school. But when I go to visit my friends, I can wear. You will go with me?"

"Sure. I'll tell Mrs. Hua that I'll need a car."

It was a little short notice for shopping but she could always say she was going to the American embassy, mere mention of which would get her the car immediately. Once out, she could direct the driver to the Friendship Store.

Would buying jeans for Qu Qing compound the case against her? She certainly had a propensity for leading youth up the garden path. Encouraging them to wear jeans! This was the depth of Western decadence!

At two o'clock the car was waiting and so was Qu Qing. Jiao Zhong En was coming through the gate. She smiled her greeting and he asked, "Where are you going?"

"We're going to town. What are you doing here?"

"I have come to see you."

"Oh. Uh . . . would you like to ride along with us?"

She felt a movement of annoyance from Qu Qing. He would not be pleased to have someone else in the car who spoke English. He always needed her undivided attention.

"I must speak with you."

"Come along. We can speak in the car."

At the door of the embassy, he followed her out and they stood out of earshot of Qu Qing. "Has something happened?"

"No. It is perhaps nothing at all. Have the police been to see you again?"

"Not since yesterday. Why?"

"They spoke to you yesterday? What did they say?"

"Do you know the cook was found dead?"

"Yes, yes. I know. The police say it was his heart." He obviously didn't think this event was noteworthy. "Did they say anything to you?"

"About what?"

He said nothing for a moment. Then: "I am afraid for you."

"For *me?*" She laughed weakly. "Why should you be afraid for me?"

"The police questioned me about you."

"What about me?"

"They wanted to know what my wife told me. About your arguments with her. If anything more had happened between you."

"What! Again? I thought we'd settled all that."

"They were not satisfied. They asked if there was physical violence between you."

She laughed. "That's ridiculous. The last time I was physically violent was when I was six years old and I scratched my brother's face."

"She said things about you—your influence on the students."

"Don't worry, I'm not about to be arrested for murder." She sounded more confident than she felt. Her conversations with the investigating officer had been civil and civilized. There had been no suggestion that he suspected her of anything. But maybe his friendliness was just a smoke screen. Maybe he had been hoping she would betray herself—that she really had killed Mrs. Li. When pretending not to understand her didn't work, maybe he thought speaking to her in her own language would make her talk a little too much . . . a revealing slip of the tongue . . . He *had* asked her if she had known Zhong En before the murder. She had thought he might be suspicious of Zhong En. Or maybe some of the other soldiers were still carrying on an investigation of their own, and theirs were the suspicions Zhong En had heard.

"They have already questioned me about my friendship with you."

"You mean the police?"

"No, not the police. The old man at the door has asked me why I come so often to the foreigner."

"Oh, does he think I corrupt adults too? Is he afraid I'll make you betray the revolution?"

He shook his head. "And the women in the office, they say it is not wise to make friends with you, that the police already . . ." He paused, as if he had said more than he wanted to.

"What about the police?"

"Nothing. The women are gossips. They do not have enough work to keep them busy, so they make up problems in other people's lives."

"What are they making up?" she insisted.

"The police are suspicious of everyone. It means nothing."

"You mean they're suspicious of you? They think you had something to do with your wife's death?"

He looked startled and then the look was gone. "I have told the security police something. I want you to know."

Her heart gave a sudden lurch.

"I told them who has reason to kill my wife."

"You know who killed your wife?"

"I do not know exactly, but I have told the police a reason. I explain it very carefully so they will believe it. Perhaps they will stop asking questions and go away."

She looked puzzled. "What are you saying, Zhong En? Do you know why your wife was murdered?"

"When they are told firmly by someone in authority that something is so, they believe it. They will think that those who have learning must know things they do not. They do not trust me as an intellectual, but they respect me, my knowledge. And you. We must give them a solution so they will leave us in peace."

"I don't know," she said doubtfully. "They don't appear all that simple to me."

"I think someone from the ministry did this; an official high in the ministry."

"Who?"

"I do not know that. Only I think it must be someone who has much to lose, who fears my wife greatly."

"Why should someone in the Education Ministry be afraid of your wife? She had no connection with the ministry."

"I will explain. You see, she knew about the tests."

That was an explanation?

"What did she know about the tests that would make someone kill her? She had nothing to do with the academic part of the college."

"No, no. It was not the tests. She had no use for the tests. She had the results. She knew who had passed and who had failed."

"So what? How could it matter that she knew a little ahead of the official announcement? People seem to know that all the time. There's always someone who 'has a friend' in the ministry."

"She knew who *really* passed and failed. Not the results that were to be announced. The real results."

"Are you saying that these examinations are rigged?"

"Rigged?"

"Dishonest. The people who pass are not the ones who are permitted to go abroad?"

"Not all those who pass are permitted to go. Only those who are approved. Also some get passing grades through the back door. They are relatives of important officials." He looked at her and shook his head in mock exasperation. "Did you not ask me how it could happen that four members of the same family could be studying at your Columbia University—a cadre and his wife and two daughters? When they question you again, tell them you have heard talk about it in the United States, that newspapers write about those visiting scholars who have not passed the examinations."

"Do you mean someone killed her because she threatened to expose him?"

"Perhaps. Perhaps she did not threaten exposure."

"What would she do with the information? Surely it wasn't worth money to anyone!"

"No, not money. In China, it is not money that is coveted, as in the United States. There is very little money here—for anyone. It is power, influence and power. That is what people want."

"But your wife wouldn't keep quiet if she knew a crime was being committed—would she?"

"Perhaps," he said again. "She did not approve of all these tests and going abroad. The knowledge of the test results could mean power for her."

"Power to do what—to get what?"

"Who knows? Power to control others. Perhaps it was for her just the knowledge that she knew, when she and the minister saw each other at a meeting. Better than money, that information."

"But why kill her if she wasn't really demanding anything?"

"One can never know when she will tell what she knows to the Central Committee, to the Party. Who knows when she might decide that her love for China required that she reveal what she knew?"

"Do the police accept this as a reasonable explanation?"

"I do not know. It is difficult to know what they believe. They reveal only what they wish to reveal. No one can tell how their investigation progresses."

He looked completely wiped out. What was the matter with him?

Was it the murder and all the questioning finally beginning to take its toll?

"What are you afraid of, Zhong En? Why are you trying to make the police accept this solution to the murder?"

"Because it is true."

"If it's true, then they'll look into it. Why are you so . . . ?" She stopped abruptly.

"No, my dear. I did not kill my wife," he said quietly. "Nor do the police think I did. That which police in your country would believe to be obvious is not obvious to these men. It is foreigners they suspect of heinous crimes. That is what they have been taught."

She walked thoughtfully up the steps of the embassy. Maybe she'd better make contact here—say something, just in case . . .

4

She bit her lip so she wouldn't be tempted to say anything to the receptionist and just signed the sheet. Then she walked firmly through the first door to the right as if she knew where she was going. The Chinese national at the first desk looked at her uncertainly. The man behind her was still typing, one laborious letter at a time.

"I'd like to see the Assistant Cultural Attaché," she told the woman at the desk. She thought that if she said it in capital letters, the way she had first heard it, she'd make an impression.

"Please?"

Oh, hell.

"The Assistant Cultural Attaché," she repeated as clearly as she knew how.

"Who?"

Enough of this, she thought. "I wish," she announced firmly, "to speak to the Ambassador."

"Who?"

"Is this the American embassy?" she asked carefully.

"Yes."

"Well, I want to speak to the person in charge."

"Who?"

She smiled vaguely into the air and made a lot of noise with her heels on the cement floor as she walked through the inner door, expecting to find the person with whom she had talked about the English-language exam. She'd probably get no satisfaction, but at least she'd be able to cuss her out in a language she understood.

Startled to see a man sitting at the desk, she started her demand at the top of the pecking order. "I want to speak to the Ambassador."

"Can you tell me what it's about, please?"

"No. It's important for me to speak to Ambassador Herron."

"Do you know the Ambassador personally?"

"Do I have to know him before I can speak to him? I'm an American and there is a problem. Isn't that what he's here for?"

"Well . . . uh . . . of course. . . . But perhaps I can help."

An embassy official she had met at a party had told her that the Ambassador saw his function in Beijing as paving the way for American businessmen to establish contacts and operations in China. Ambassador Herron cared not one cent's worth for American teachers in China. As for tourists who were not wealthy industrialists, they could all be swallowed up in the Ming Tombs for all he cared. He spoke to no one who didn't have a plan for establishing an American telephone company the length of the Great Wall. He was looking to his future too; he would not always be an ambassador.

"What is your position here?"

"I'm the First Assistant Attaché in charge of Cultural Relations. *Is* there something I can do for you?" His voice had an edge of impatience. He must be very busy. How many assistant attachés in charge of cultural relations were needed to sit at desks in this outpost of American civilization?

"Do you mind if I sit down?" She sat without waiting for an answer. She didn't get one anyhow. "I don't know if you've heard, but there was a murder on the campus of the college where I teach."

He was properly horrified.

"The police are investigating and . . ." She stopped. How to put this without causing the man to suspect that she had any connection with the crime? "I'm beginning to feel as if I should have some protection . . . uh . . . some backup in case . . ." This wasn't sounding right at all. "What if they accuse me of the murder?" she blurted out. And was immediately appalled at what she had said.

The First Assistant Attaché in charge of Cultural Relations sat there staring, with his mouth open. One of the Americans who tottered in here every day with an amazing variety of complaints had finally flipped.

"An American was murdered?"

"No, a Chinese. But the foreigners living on campus are being questioned. I'm one of them."

"Is there any reason for them to suspect one of the foreigners?"

"None of us liked the woman who was murdered."

He stared.

"No, I didn't kill her."

"Oh, I didn't . . . For goodness' sake, I wouldn't . . . I never . . ."

"I just wanted the embassy to know what was happening, in case."

"In case?"

"Well, I don't want to be caught in the bureaucratic machinery here. I know what can happen in the States. Here, not understanding the system or the language, God knows what could happen." She suddenly felt very much alone here, ten thousand miles from home. But this man had neither comfort nor advice for her. What a dumb waste of time.

"Just take my name and address so you'll have it if you need it." She scribbled the information and left.

"Yes, yes."

But the First Assistant etc., etc. was talking to her back.

5

Jiao Zhong En and Janet spent the rest of the afternoon in her room. She practiced writing Chinese characters while he leaned over her and kissed her neck from time to time. The maid at the door with a single fresh towel put a stop to that.

They discussed her impressions of China and what she would tell the people back home. Between impressions he kissed her, and although she tried to push the business of the afternoon from her mind, she responded uneasily. The doorman came to call her to the telephone. No one answered by the time she got to it.

Jiao Zhong En produced a copy of one of her books that a colleague of his proposed to translate into Chinese. *Patterns of Interaction in Contemporary Human Relations* would never make the best-seller list, but she had a certain reputation in her field and she was pleased by the recognition.

"A book of mine in Chinese! I'd love it!"

It was not until after he had left that she remembered that China ignored the international copyright agreements.

They were sitting in the easy chairs sipping sherry when Luo Geng, Mrs. Hua's elder son, came by. Mrs. Hua had brought him to her soon after her arrival in China and they met occasionally, he supposedly to practice his English, she to learn Chinese. His English was excellent and he was bored to death with her Chinese. What both Mrs. Hua and her son wanted was an American connection, so she went along with it.

Zhong En excused himself to wash for dinner and left Luo Geng to get to whatever was on his mind. "Perhaps you will help me when you return to your country," he said.

"Are you so sure you passed the examination?" she teased him.

He jerked, startled, and half-looked over his shoulder. "No, no, I am not sure. I hope I passed the examination. It is possible I did not."

"I was only joking, Luo Geng. Relax. I'm sure you did very well."

"One cannot be sure of passing until one is informed by the ministry."

"I know. I'll be glad to help you if I can. What can I do?"

"When I complete my thesis, if you would read it and give me your advice. Then you can give it to someone in your university who will invite me to the United States."

"Sure, but the only advice I can give you is about the grammar and word usage. I don't know anything about economics. I've told you that."

"Yes, you know. You have helped me much with ideas."

She could feel the familiar rush of impatience. Just because she was an American, that meant she was an expert on all things American. She couldn't get him to accept the fact that she simply was ignorant when it came to economic theories and practices. "I'll do what I can to help you continue your studies in the United States, okay?"

"If I am sent by my government, I will go." He was more cautious than some of the other students she had talked to.

"I have no special influence, you know. All you can do is apply to a university for admission."

He plainly didn't believe her. A university professor who had been permitted to come to China for a whole year was obviously a person with influence. He left when Zhong En came back. She wondered if Mrs. Hua was fluttering around somewhere in the vicinity waiting to hear what Janet had told her son.

6

Dinner was fish with so many small bones that eating it gave one a sense of great danger. She was afraid to talk and eat at the same time.

She introduced Jiao Zhong En to the others, although some of them had met him. Then the talk swirled around—in English, French, Swahili, and Chinese.

"Does the food seem better to you?" Haji asked the table at large.

"You know, it *is* better," said Colette. "Who is doing the cooking?"

"Yun Fung, I think." She was the woman who usually served up the food, always with an apologetic look.

Sally coughed and all eyes turned on her expectantly.

"Are you all right?" Janet asked.

"It's all right. It wasn't a bone."

One of the young dining-room workers came up to the table and hovered.

"This food is very good," Ka Ka Chi told him.

He beamed and went to tell Yun Fung. They could see her in the kitchen, smiling and nodding.

"I am wondering which one of us would have killed him if he had not died." Masomakali seemed to have recovered from his panic at the prospect of losing the services of the cook. Had he found another source of supply?

Some of them started to laugh and then stopped, remembering that a murderer was still at large, and that the husband of the murdered woman was sitting at the table with them.

"Were the police here all day today?" Colette asked. "I have been with my teacher the whole day."

No one knew. The African students had been in class all day. Sally taught only in the mornings; afternoons she was off on her bicycle exploring the city. She had announced early that she didn't want to waste all her time teaching.

Colette called the young worker back to the table and asked him. He nodded. One soldier had come to talk to the women who sold the food tickets. They had talked in the office for a short time. He did not know what was discussed.

His eyes wandered nervously in Janet's direction.

Masomakali guffawed. "Hah! He does not know! As soon as the soldier was gone, the women told everyone! I would wager my life!" He spoke in the French dialect that Janet could not understand, and Colette translated.

Janet felt very uneasy. Had the boy been looking at her or at Zhong En? Well, what if he had? Dammit! She was acting as if she had something to be afraid of. She was getting as paranoid as everyone else in this country. She had done nothing wrong. No matter what the gossip was or what the authorities didn't like about her, she was still an American. Even in China they wouldn't assume she was guilty just on the basis of rumor and foreignness.

And what about Wang Qu Qing? her conscience asked her. Jeans and American checks to lead him from the path of righteousness! *Did* she have something to be afraid of?

XING QI SI—THURSDAY

1

Another sightseeing trip. This time classes were called off and everyone came along. Only Yue Zhen, who had mentioned last night that her baby was not well, was missing.

The Imperial Palace is an awesome collection of buildings and courts. Beautiful carved teak screens and furniture fill the rooms. There are sculptures of gold and precious gems and doorframes of colorful mosaic tiles. Janet thought it would take a year to go through it and see everything there was to see.

Even on a weekday the place was packed with people. Whole
families roamed from room to room, adults lifting the infants over
the foot-high stone thresholds, and gazing with appreciation at the
vestiges of their ancient past, content that they were not appreciat-
ing the works of the hated mandarins. To them these beautiful
artifacts were only additional evidence that throughout the ages the
workers have always been hardworking, skillful, and clever, even
when they were most sorely oppressed.

People looked at her. She was the only female wearing a skirt, and
the bright colors were a startling contrast to the sea of gray, blue,
and white. Only the toddlers had brightly colored pants and ribbons
in their hair.

There were hundreds of toddlers, shepherded by doting parents.
Those who were not yet toilet-trained had the crotches cut out of
their pants and nothing on underneath. No worry about diapers!

Mr. Guo, who had, as usual, planned the trip and was acting as
translator, disappeared for a moment into one of the shops that
circled the inner courtyard and came back with a bottle of Coca-
Cola for her. *Ke Kou Ke Le*—Tasty Happiness. The Chinese preferred orange soda, and when she told her students that most Americans drank the stuff, they could hardly believe it.

"Is there something wrong, Mr. Guo?" He was standing in the
middle of the court watching a family group that was playing with a
baby who waddled and fell among the legs of the sightseers, picking
himself up and laughing with delight as his father chased after him.

"Mr. Guo!"

"Yes, Professor. I see child."

"Yes. How is your child feeling today? Is he over his fever?"

"My child is ill."

"Oh, I'm sorry. He's not feeling better today?"

"I do not know. My wife have brought her to doctor."

"I thought your baby was a boy."

"Yes, a boy."

She sighed, but persisted. "He'll be all right, Mr. Guo. Your wife
said it wasn't serious."

"My child has died."

"What! Oh no, Mr. Guo, you don't mean that!" It was his English.
He couldn't be announcing the sudden death of his baby in this
casual way!

"Yes. Since five years." He looked inestimably forlorn.

She couldn't continue to stroll along, oohing and aahing at exotic relics, if he was going to say things like that and she was going to have to decode them. "Let's sit down for a few minutes, shall we?" She urged him over to a step out of the way of the people going into the palace.

"I think you are tired," he announced. She didn't bother to deny it.

"You had another child, Mr. Guo?"

"Yes. A boy child also. He has died."

"How terrible! How did it happen?"

"He was very ill. My wife too. They have died, two."

"Too?"

"My wife and my child."

They sat silently as she tried to sort it out. "You were married before, Mr. Guo?" she asked gently.

"I have son. He is very ill. Fever. He dies. My wife, she dies too. She has fever as my son."

"I'm so sorry." The conventional sentiment seemed lame in the face of such tragedy. No wonder he rarely smiled. How easy it had been to make fun of a serious young man who murdered the English language with such oblivious pomposity. Tears came to her eyes.

"Now my child is ill."

"Oh, Mr. Guo," she tried to reassure him. "He just has a little cold. Yue Zhen told me it wasn't serious. She said she would take him to the doctor today to get some medicine. She was sure he was going to be fine."

"He is ill many times. Perhaps he will die too."

She was shocked at the resigned acceptance. "He's just had the usual children's illnesses. He seems to be a healthy baby." She could almost see his depression deepening in the way his body sagged, the way his head seemed to be too heavy for him to hold up. "Come on, Mr. Guo, let's look at the palace. You promised to tell me about its history." She tried to pull him back to his enormous sense of official responsibility, groaning inwardly as she encouraged him in his favorite pastime. He would tell her *all* about its history, and she would understand about two percent of what he said. He was especially interested in all the old stories and myths about emperors and their wives and royal offspring. An odd fascination in so dedicated a communist.

She would crown the day with a massive headache. She could already feel the first twinges over her right eye.

At noon the faculty and students went off to get their lunch in a workers' restaurant, while Janet, Guo, Mrs. Hua, and Sally were treated to a sumptuous banquet in the private dining room of a restaurant that catered to tourists. When they all met again after lunch, no one seemed to resent the difference in treatment. That's just the way it was, and students and faculty cheerfully resumed their enthusiastic sightseeing, enjoying the grandeur and beauty of their culture as much as any tourist.

2

At four o'clock they dropped her and Sally off at the Foreign Students Building. When she saw Laura waiting for them, Mrs. Hua got off the bus too. Laura seemed very nervous. Wang Qu Qing hovered in the background waiting to be noticed.

"Laura! Why are you here?" Mrs. Hua smiled and made it sound like a greeting—almost.

"I've come to visit my friends." She sounded defiant. Was it just an American's automatic response to an attempt to control her? Or was there something more in the defiance and nervousness?

"You do not come to visit me." The teasing was unusually heavy-handed for Mrs. Hua. She was much more subtle than that.

"I'm sorry." Laura breathed a sigh of resignation and said nothing more. The silence lengthened and made them all uncomfortable.

"Come along in." Janet began to bustle. "Let's have a drink before dinner. You're staying for dinner, aren't you, Laura?"

Laura nodded. She looked very unhappy.

"Mrs. Hua, would you like to come in?"

"Yes, thank you. Just for a little while. I must go home soon."

Janet waved to Wang Qu Qing. "I am waiting for my friend," he explained.

The doorman looked carefully at them, noting the presence of the Chinese woman among the foreigners.

In her room Janet began to talk about the Imperial Palace. No one seemed interested, but it was preferable to just sitting in silence. Laura had come for a reason but she wasn't about to say anything while her cousin was there.

Finally Mrs. Hua could delay no longer. She had to shop for her family's dinner. "Come with me, Laura. Have dinner in my home."

"No, thank you. I'll come another time."

"We are your family, Laura. We care for you."

Laura looked at her steadily. "I know. I'm not likely to forget that." They were silent for a while, their eyes on each other. Mrs. Hua was not smiling. Then she said her goodbyes and left.

Laura breathed a deep sigh.

"Is there something wrong, Laura?" Janet asked her.

"No, no. Nothing wrong. It's just that families can sometimes be too much, especially Chinese families."

"How's your boyfriend?"

Her face lit up. "He's great! The nicest person I've ever met."

"What does he look like?" asked Sally.

"Oh, he's not very tall. He has a beautiful smile. And he's very intelligent."

"It sounds as if everything is working out for you." Janet looked at her a little quizzically.

"Have the police been here?"

"Today? I don't know. We've been away all day. Why? Have you heard something?"

"The examination results came out today."

"So? Why should the police be interested in those?"

"They shouldn't!" she said quickly. "I don't know."

She wasn't making sense. Janet took another tack. "Do you know anyone who passed?" Last year's English class had taken the test, as well as a couple of faculty members.

"About half of those who took it. My cousins passed."

"Mrs. Hua's sons? Both of them?"

"Yes."

"Well, that's good. Why didn't you tell Mrs. Hua?"

Laura shook her head. "She knows. She'll know soon."

An interesting slip of the tongue. Janet's eyebrows rose.

Laura jumped up. "I can't stay for dinner," she said abruptly. "I've got to get back. Thanks for the drink." And she was gone.

Sally and Janet looked at each other. "That was odd. What's bothering her?"

"Nothing. She just wants to get back to her boyfriend." Sally grinned in sympathy. *That* was something she could understand!

Janet had been quite sure that Luo Geng, Mrs. Hua's elder son, would pass the English test because he spoke and wrote very well, but she was surprised about Fa Ping, the younger one. Even though her own French was weak, she could tell that he could not speak the language at all. Were there so few candidates for France that even a low grade would get him through? Did this puzzle have something to do with Laura's peculiar behavior? It had been almost as if she was afraid to talk too much about the tests. Did she know something that was making her afraid?

Laura had trembled and almost collapsed when she had learned that Mrs. Li had been murdered. She seemed to be walking a thin line on the edge of panic. Why?

3

After dinner Wang Qu Qing was still hanging around outside. He smiled broadly when he saw Janet. "Hello," he said, "I am here."

She grinned back at him. "I'm glad to see you. Have you had your dinner?"

"Yes. I go to eat and I come back. Do you know who passed the examination to go to United States?"

She didn't want to spoil his fun. "No. Who?"

"Luo Geng, the son of Mrs. Hua."

"Oh, that's fine! I'm very happy for him."

"And also Fa Ping, the younger son of Mrs. Hua. He has passed the examination." He was making the most of his news, drawing it out for effect.

Janet nodded. "Are you here to practice your French? Colette isn't here."

"It does not matter. I will speak English."

She smiled at him and thought how much she liked him. This was the future of the world, no matter which country you were in. The bright, rebellious, irrepressible spirit.

Ching Mei came up with Zhu Mei and Dawang, and Janet walked to the bench with them. The young women were usually first to arrive to practice their English. Zhu Mei, who had learned to play the violin so she could join the army, was, as usual, the enterprising one. She was all ready with an English sentence: "Did you have a good time today?"

"Yes, thank you. Very good."

"You go to the Imperial Palace," said Dawang.

"That's right. It was beautiful. And how are you all today?"

Ching Mei answered. "I am fine." She seemed fine too. No haunting memories today of the depredations of the Cultural Revolution.

"Good!" Janet encouraged her. "What did you do today?"

She looked questioningly at her friends, who started to translate.

"No!" Janet said in mock anger. "No Chinese spoken here."

They laughed, and she tried again. "What . . . did . . . you . . . do . . . today?"

Ching Mei looked blank for a moment and then the light came. "I! I go to class!"

Janet, sitting facing the building entrance, saw the army jeep pull up and the officer in charge of the investigation come toward the group. "Good evening," he said.

She wondered if the students would be silent with him there, although they didn't look disturbed by his presence.

"Did you want to speak to me?"

"I am here to practice my English too," he said seriously.

Everyone smiled. "You speak English very well," Zhu Mei told him.

There were no wiseacres here, ready to bait a cop the way American college students might have.

"Have you found the one who killed Comrade Li?" asked Wang Qu Qing.

This was temerity even for him. They might not be afraid of the soldiers of the People's Liberation Army, but they were surely circumspect in their approach to authorities.

"Not yet. But the killer will be found."

"Many people did not love her."

"Perhaps. Did *you* not love her?"

The question did not faze him. "She was not welcoming the professor."

"And for that you were angry, because she did not welcome the professor?"

"The professor comes to China to teach us. All to welcome her."

"Yes, you are right. You came here on the day Comrade Li was murdered?"

"Yes. I come every day. I practice to speak English. Also French when the Frenchwoman is here."

"You went up to visit your friend?"

"Yes, Petiri. We eat and then we come out."

"Did you see Comrade Li?"

"No, I do not think I see her." He said it reluctantly. He hated to admit absolutely that he hadn't seen or heard something. "Jiao Zhong En is here."

The officer nodded, as if this was not news to him.

"Were you also here on the day of the murder?" he asked Ching Mei casually.

She looked at him blankly, startled into forgetting what little English she knew.

Janet interceded. "She doesn't know very much English."

For some reason, perhaps in deference to her, he chose not to speak Chinese. "You were here Thursday?" he asked again.

"Thursday?"

Janet translated automatically, surprising herself. Nobody noticed.

"I here," Ching Mei answered.

"You saw Li?"

"I not see." She pointed to the side of the building. But she was out of her depth again. She said something in Chinese and the officer replied. She spoke again.

When they had finished, Wang Qu Qing asked, "Will you question all of us now?"

She saw Mr. Xu coming slowly from the gate, and when he caught sight of the soldier, he hesitated, but then came on. Had he told the officer that his daughter had seen Jiao Zhong En and Ching Mei walk to the rear of the building after Mrs. Li? She thought probably not; he wouldn't give such information unsolicited, especially when a friend was involved. Perhaps Jiao Zhong En had told him. Now he asked only if any of them had information that might help him in his investigation. They hadn't.

4

The officer remained after the students had dispersed to their studying and Mr. Xu had gone home. "Did you understand what Ching Mei told me?" he asked.

"No."

"She did not speak to Mrs. Li, but she heard her in an argument."

"How did you know she was there at that time?"

"I questioned everyone in the building who has windows from which the Foreign Students Building can be seen. There was a witness who saw the girl walk behind the building."

"Surely you never thought that child had anything to do with the murder!"

"She is twenty years old. And she blames Mrs. Li and others like her for the disgrace of her father and the death of her mother. An old hatred, yes, but it is always possible."

"What was she doing there, did she tell you?"

"She walks where you do, to the building on the other side. She also has friends there."

There was a pause. Then he said, "You do not wish to know who was with Mrs. Li?"

"Yes," she said weakly. "Who?"

"Jiao Zhong En, her husband."

She felt sick. She didn't want to hear any more.

"He came to ask the women in the office where his wife was. They told him she had just left the building. He knew her practice of looking at the progress of the construction, so he looked for her in the back."

"He told you?"

"Yes," he said drily. "He told us when we told him." He sighed. "If people would tell us the truth, matters would progress more quickly."

"He's a good man," she defended him.

"The good also lie, is that not so?"

"Okay, you win."

"Pardon?"

She shook her head. "What was the argument about?" Then added, to be politic, "Can you tell me?"

"They argued about their daughter."

"Yue Zhen? What about her?"

He looked at her reproachfully. "You know I do not mean Yue Zhen. I mean Yanmin, the one who works in the dining room."

"Oh." It was a very small voice.

"Is it not important that Mrs. Li kept this secret from her husband, that he is the father of the girl?"

"Yes. I'm sorry, I . . ."

He waved her words away. "I think you would not protect someone you believed to be a murderer."

"I wouldn't. I don't think Jiao Zhong En would kill anyone."

"Perhaps. But he was very angry that day. His wife would not stay home to hear him, so he came to look for her. He did not want his daughter to do this kind of work. He wanted her to be educated. He says when he left she was alive. That someone must have come after him to kill her."

"Do you believe him?"

"I do not know. But if we accept his story then we know that Li was still alive a few minutes after five."

"A few minutes after five? I thought Jiao saw her about six-forty!"

"Where did you learn that?"

"Uh . . . I thought . . . uh . . . he was seen . . ."

"Who saw him then, at six-forty?" he demanded.

"I must be mistaken," she said weakly. "I just got the time wrong."

He looked at her soberly and she had trouble meeting his eyes. She wondered why he continued to be so friendly when he knew she wasn't being completely candid with him. Maybe he was relying on her to tell him the salient facts as her "intuition" discovered them. She hoped this was it—and not that he was just giving her enough rope to hang herself.

She thought about the sequence of events after Mrs. Li had left the Foreign Students Building to make her rounds. First her husband had followed to argue with her. When her husband left, the cook went to have his little session of threats and counter-threats.

Then the murderer left his calling card. Then the cook again, being sick. All this within half an hour. And then Jiao again more than an hour later. How did they all miss seeing each other? It sounded like a choreographed Marx Brothers comedy.

XING QI WU—FRIDAY

1

"The police, they think I have killed Mrs. Li."

"Qu Qing, I can't talk now. I've got preparations to make for my class." She tried to push past him and get into the classroom.

"Ah, you do not believe me. You think I make up stories, like a foolish child."

"No. I don't think you're a foolish child." What a foolish child he is, she thought. No matter how intelligent they were, they seemed to stay young so much longer in China. It must have something to do with the restrictions on movement.

"I *could* have killed her. I had the . . . uh . . . motive and the . . . uh . . . opportunity."

That stopped her in her tracks. She stared at him. Then it struck her. "You've been reading those detective stories I gave you!"

The official Chinese policy lumped such literature with pornography. Maybe the cadres were right; maybe these kids *were* too impressionable for such reading. "Why do you think the police suspect you? Have they questioned you?"

"Last night, you heard. He asks me if I do not love Comrade Li. He thinks maybe I kill her."

"This is not a game, Qu Qing. The person who killed her will be tried and maybe executed. You wouldn't want to be accused of such a crime." She looked at him sternly.

"Do you think Ching Mei did the crime?"

"No, I don't. And neither does anyone else. I think we had better stop talking about it. Don't you have a class this morning?"

"Yes, I must go soon. Comrade Li denounces Ching Mei's father in Cultural Revolution. Ching Mei is small child that time, but her father tells her. Maybe she kills the old Li."

"Mrs. Li denounced her father? I thought Ching Mei and her family lived down south. I didn't know she had ever met Mrs. Li before."

"Oh, well, perhaps it was not Mrs. Li who puts *das bao* to her father. But Mrs. Li does this to many people, so Ching Mei hates her."

Janet had a vision of men and women, enormous signs hanging from their necks describing their crimes against the revolution. She shuddered.

"Qu Qing, enough! Many people had reason to dislike Mrs. Li. Ching Mei is very sad about what happened to her family but that doesn't mean she's capable of murder. I've been slowly starving to death in the Foreign Students Building but that doesn't mean I would kill someone." The hell it doesn't. One more week of that food and I *would* have killed someone. "The police will find who did it soon and that will be the end of it."

"I think you will discover who did it. Colette says you will be the one. Also, your students say this."

She sighed. "At the moment, I don't know any more than the police do."

"The police!" he said with disdain. "They are peasants. You are a professor."

"Go, Qu Qing. I'll see you tonight."

He grinned. "Goodbye, Professor. *À bientot!*" He gave a small bow and left. She could not help smiling after him.

Mr. Guo and Yue Zhen came into the classroom together. Today they had their baby with them and Yue Zhen hastened to explain why she had not left him with the aunt. "My baby is ill. I will take him to doctor. But I come to class first. It is all right?"

"Yes, Yue Zhen." She patted the baby's face and made a sound that one makes at babies, but the poor child looked at her listlessly. His nose was stopped up and he sneezed. He really wasn't feeling well. The three of them huddled together, looking miserable.

"I tell go now. Not class," Guo said. "Must wait long time for doctor."

"Doctor tells me yesterday to give medicine to child. I give."

"Did he tell you to bring the baby back to see him today?"

"No. Not today. Not time for medicine to make better."

"Then why do you have the baby out? Why are you taking him to the doctor?"

She shrugged and looked at her husband. He was the one who wouldn't give the medicine time to work.

"The baby would probably be better off tucked up in a warm bed," Janet told them.

"I say to doctor." He was the man of the family and his word was law. "Child very ill. If child dies . . ." His voice did not falter; he just stopped talking.

"I will go now." Yue Zhen looked at him and turned to leave.

"Would you like to go with her, Mr. Guo?" She thought the doctor might be able to reassure him about the baby's condition.

But he insisted on staying. Here at the college he could maintain some sense of control. In his small sphere of influence he could order events as he wished. Wife and child: to doctor; letters to translate: six; tours to arrange: two; foreigners to conduct through college: three. All predictable, all manageable by him. No doctor to say the baby's illness was out of control, that nothing more could be done. No death, against which there was no power great enough. Mr. Guo was a small authoritarian in a small world. He could take orders from cadres and carry them out without question. To those below him, he could give orders and he expected them to be followed without question. Outside the parameters of his world he was a helpless and very frightened man.

"I'm sure the baby will be all right, Mr. Guo," she said as he took his seat. "He just has a bad cold. The medicine the doctor prescribed should help."

He didn't hear her attempts to comfort him. How could someone who held his head so stiff and erect still manage to look so wretched?

2

Mr. Xu had the time to come to class today. "Hello, Professor." He smiled and bowed. "Zhong En and I will take you to see beautiful temple."

"You will?" Not even a question: Would you like to see the temple? Just the assumption that she was ready whenever anybody else made a decision. "I'm not sure I want to see another temple right now, Mr. Xu."

"Yes, you will want to see this temple. It is very beautiful." He smiled broadly. "There are not so many now as before the Cultural Revolution. Many were destroyed. This one is still beautiful. You will see."

She gave up. "Okay. Thanks, Mr. Xu. It's very nice of you. Who else will be going?"

"Jiao and I, that is all."

"No one else from the college?"

"This is short trip. I have arranged for car and there is room only for three."

"No."

"You will not go?" He was very surprised.

"No, I will not go."

As if he knew what she was thinking—as if *she* knew what she was thinking—he said, "This is as the day the emperor built it. Very little needed to make beautiful again. Many people come there to see."

"I'm very tired, Mr. Xu." That should do it.

"It is not necessary to walk. It is very small temple, but very beautiful." He looked hurt and disappointed. Requisitioning a car and a driver could not have been easy for him. He had arranged a gift and she was throwing it back in his face. And she wasn't even sure why she was doing it.

"Okay, Mr. Xu," she said reluctantly. And, as an afterthought: "It's very nice of you to arrange it."

The Temple of Heaven was the most breathtakingly exquisite structure she had ever seen. She knew immediately that no words, no photograph, no painting, could do justice to the perfect harmony of the three-tiered, fluted, turquoise-blue pagoda, the earth out of which it rose, and the sky that framed it. They told her it was a monument to the harvest, that emperors had come here to give thanks for the fruitfulness of the earth. She was not surprised to learn that the objective of the builders had been to achieve just that harmony that flowed into her.

Going through the rooms of the temple was anticlimactic. She kept walking out and down the stone steps so that she could gaze up at it again and again. In a land of temples, it was matchless.

She took her eyes away from it for a moment and saw the two friends standing a little distance away, speaking earnestly. They were very fond of each other, both quiet, soft-spoken men. They had both endured personal suffering in China's upheavals, and had emerged clinging to their belief in people and their faith in the power of learning. She liked them very much. The warmth she felt for Jiao Zhong En was firmly based on her liking him. She caught her breath as she remembered his kisses. Oh yes. Warmth was the word.

The descending sun now was glancing off the gold ball that adorned the center of the top tier of the temple. She let the perfect harmony of the picture flow through her. It soothed her soul. The vague doubts she had were dissipated in the beauty of the scene. It was just that old devil, foreign experts' paranoia, nudging to displace her good sense. She would not succumb to it.

3

They walked off the grounds and sat for a few minutes on a bench nearby. Small shops lined the street, and tourists crowded in to buy everything from cheap china figurines of mandarins to intricately worked cloisonné vases that demonstrated one of China's ancient crafts.

"I'm glad you made me come here today. It was good to get away from the college."

"Yes," said Mr. Xu. "But we do not forget, Zhong En. We are sad for you." He put his hand on his friend's arm.

Zhong En nodded. "It is over. Let there be an end to it all."

"It's not over yet. Don't you want them to find the killer?"

"For what purpose? She is gone. He will not kill again."

Many people would consider such a sentiment evidence of guilty knowledge—at least. But she knew what he meant. "Yes, you're probably right. Few murderers kill more than once. A driving motive, the one person who provokes it, the seized opportunity. Not like the murder novels we read in the West, where one murder almost invariably leads to another."

"Is that correct?" Xu asked.

Zhong En nodded. "That is so."

"But punishment is another matter. Don't you want the murderer punished?"

"The one who kills is himself a victim. And he suffers for killing—perhaps his whole life."

She wondered if he would be so objective if he had loved his wife. Brittle, she reproved herself. A very brittle response to a rational point of view. "Even if I didn't tell anyone else, I'd want to know. Just to finish the matter, to end it without the question unanswered."

"Perhaps we will never know."

"And you're satisfied with that?"

"Yes," he said simply.

"But people are under suspicion. I am—and both of you. I wouldn't want that suspicion floating around forever."

"Do you mean you suspect Zhong En because of what my daughter said? She is a child; she only thinks she sees Zhong En walk behind the building that night. It was dark. She is mistaken. I will speak to her again about this."

"Ah, my friend, it is not necessary to be harsh with the child. She did see me when I went back to speak to my wife." For the first time since it had happened, he was visibly upset.

"Zhong En, do not distress yourself. It is over. Say no more."

Was Xu warning his friend? About what? Not to say too much to her? Not to betray himself?

"There is nothing to hide, Xu my friend. You are both my friends. Janet knows what I recently discovered—that Yanmin is my child."

"The officer told me that you had a fight with your wife that night about the education of your daughter. But that was at five o'clock. Li Hua says she saw you at six-forty."

"No, my wife did not fight. She made her decision and would listen to no argument. When she decided something, she never changed. She believed that the principles of the revolution made her decisions the only right ones. She had decided how this child must live her life and there was to be no discussion. After she told me about Yanmin, she tried not to see me alone. Each evening she did not come home until it was very late so that I could not speak to her, try to change her mind. I came to find her, to try to talk to her. But she would not listen."

He didn't mention the discrepancy in time.

"There was no way to move her. That night I pleaded with her. There was nothing I could do."

"Now there's no one in Yanmin's way. She'll be able to do whatever she wants."

Zhong En shook his head. "It is too late."

She could feel her jaw tighten with impatience. "But less than two weeks ago you were arguing that the girl should be educated! Now it's already too late? That doesn't make sense."

She almost saw the leap Xu made to defend his friend. "The girl believes as her mother did. Who can change her?"

"Maybe her father can. He'll never know until he tries."

Zhong En just kept shaking his head. Xu looked at him sadly.

4

The murder was shared. The thought sprang into Janet's head. Shared.

One person strangles; the other says, We share the responsibility —and stabs.

Two dear friends? Two friends who have also shared profound grief before this?

It was not until they were back in the car that Janet came out of her reverie to say, "I think I know why Mrs. Li was stabbed after she was strangled."

The men looked at each other. She was conscious of a sudden stillness in the car. Bulling his way through the masses of pedestrians and bicycles, the driver kept his hand on the horn, and the incessant sound wrapped itself around the three of them, shutting them into the hush.

Sitting in the back seat with a man on either side, she began to feel uncomfortable—closed in. Zhong En's hand covered hers and the pressure of his fingers on her ring began to hurt. Xu seemed to move closer, his face just a breath from hers.

Suddenly, Xu's arm swung out toward her just as the car brakes screeched, and she saw the right door implode in slow motion. She was thrown sideways and slid to the floor, banging her head against the front seat. A roar of voices rose outside as she half lay against the seat, stunned. Above the noise she could hear the frantic voice of the driver start at the moment of impact from the only other car within a hundred miles.

Xu reached for her. Terrified, she flailed at him, fighting him off. Then Zhong En's hands grabbed her arms and began to pull her up. She was powerless between them.

The unintelligible voices got louder and louder, feeding her terror. Somehow she managed to touch the left door handle, but a jerk from Zhong En caused her fingers to scrabble down. She opened her mouth to scream.

A gust of cool air and a single authoritative voice stopped all the sound and motion. A face wearing a khaki cap with a red star on it was poked through the door. Janet felt a measure of sanity returning, although her heart pounded wildly. She wasn't hurt and the others seemed all right too. She couldn't get herself to object when Jiao Zhong En insisted they could drive home without assistance. He assured the soldier that they would stop at the campus clinic to be checked. A beauty of a shiner was starting around the driver's left eye and halfway down his cheek, but he wanted to drive. He started to talk again and gesticulate wildly, and he never stopped until he dropped her off at the Foreign Students Building.

5

Students and faculty had unlimited access to the small hospital/clinic near the gate of the college compound. The place was very old but clean, without the exaggerated trappings of pseudo-sterility seen in American hospitals. The five or six doctors and attendants wore wrinkled white gowns; a couple wore surgical masks which they removed to greet the new patients. In attendance were a specialist in acupuncture, a traditional physician, and a doctor of Western medicine. They all asked to be checked by the traditionalist—as most Chinese patients did.

The pharmacopoeia of the traditionalist was fascinating to the Westerner. A pharmacy had all the walls lined with wooden drawers, in each of which was a different dried herb or grain or flower ready to be ground and distilled into medicine for a specific complaint. Each patient came away with a small bottle of concentrated liquid. At home he boiled water, added a spoonful or two of the concentrate and drank to his health. When the bottle was finished he returned to have the prescription refilled or, lacking the hoped-for improvement, for rediagnosis.

Janet chattered animatedly on the short drive from the clinic to the Foreign Students Building. "That was an interesting experience! So different from an American clinic. The people were so kind. And we didn't even have to wait! I understand the students are treated free of charge." She carried her bottle of medicine like a souvenir, resolved to take it back to the States to illustrate her description of Chinese medical treatment.

As long as she talked she didn't have to meet her friends' eyes.

6

That night Zhong En came bringing a bag of tangerines, as if she were an invalid. The fruit had just come to the markets and she had once told him that fresh fruit and vegetables were what she missed most in China. Although China produced more vegetables than the United States and the Soviet Union combined, Janet sometimes thought the total crop must be cabbage.

He kissed her when he closed the door behind him, as if they had been lovers for a long time. She disengaged herself abruptly. What had happened in the car? Had the menace been real?

He seemed to misunderstand her action. Motioning toward the window and the people in the courtyard, he smiled. "I no longer worry about being seen. I feel as if you are a part of me."

"Zhong En, was your wife dead when you walked out back the second time?"

"Yes," he said after a silence. "I found her that way."

"Why didn't you say anything?" She didn't sound accusatory—only wanting to know.

He shook his head. "I saw her and I wanted only to be away from there. I did not want to see more, or to speak of it. I wanted only to be away," he said again.

"But the police know you said nothing . . ."

He smiled a little. "They know I am not a man who takes events in his own hands. Whatever happens . . ." His voice trailed off and he shrugged.

"Did you see Ching Mei behind you?"

"I saw her—both times. Each time she turned off to walk on the path in front of the unfinished building. She could not see what I saw."

She looked at him speculatively. "I still find it hard to believe that you don't care to know who could have done this. That you don't want the person to be discovered and punished."

He smiled again. "My poor Janet, we are truly worlds apart. You will never know the patience that we Chinese have cultivated for thousands of years."

"I don't know if it's patience. It begins to look to me much more like resignation."

"Oh no," he said very calmly. "It is patience. Look at our history: a very patient people who finally overthrew the mandarins. A very patient people who endured for ten years and then, with one blow, stopped the ravaging of the Gang of Four. Patience may appear to be resignation—until the final day. And then it is clear to all that it really was a waiting all along."

She had a sudden vision of a billion people going about their daily lives, experiencing their thousand daily frustrations, and waiting . . . waiting . . .

Had Jiao also waited? Waited . . . ?

7

She shook off the thought and busied herself with making tea. When he came up behind her and tried to put his arms around her waist she moved quickly to avoid him and spoke as if nothing was the matter. "The police seem to be waiting too. They just keep questioning everyone again and again, going over the same ground. It's a kind of waiting for things to happen, instead of looking for evidence."

"It may be more effective than all the modern technology of your police. People betray themselves." He sounded sad, but not as if he was talking about himself.

"Zhong En, do you know who killed your wife?" She could feel her heart pound while she waited for him to answer. She tried to justify the question to herself: he didn't want the murderer apprehended. He was not frightened for himself. He had made up that ludicrous story about a corrupt minister, pretending he was worried about her. And now he was waiting, certain that whoever it was was bound to betray himself—or herself.

He started to put his arms around her, but she pushed him away, still waiting for him to answer. "You do not think I am the one?" Very quiet.

"N-no. No, I don't. I really don't." She had to bite her lip to keep from saying it over and over. There was no way she could feel love for a man who had murdered his wife. Didn't everyone believe she was intuitive about people? Wasn't she an excellent psychologist? What the hell was the matter with her?

Her breath came out on a sob and she was afraid she was going to cry. Of all the silly, weak-kneed, unscientific . . . ! She reached for the sherry bottle and poured, slopping it over the rims of the glasses. With her back to Zhong En she leaned on the table and got herself together. When she turned back to him she looked calm. But she knew he had answered her question.

Xɪɴɢ Qɪ Yɪ—Mᴏɴᴅᴀʏ

1

She had hardly begun to relax after lunch when the police came to her door and called her out. Mrs. Hua was there too. It was not a good sign if the officer had brought an official interpreter with him. As if he spoke no English, he told something to Mrs. Hua in Chinese.

"He would like you to go with them." Mrs. Hua pointed to the jeep with the two soldiers sitting up front.

"Go where?"

"Uh . . . to . . . to the . . . to the headquarters." Her voice was even softer than usual.

Janet spoke directly to the officer, forcing him to look at her. "Why, you're crazy! You don't mean you seriously believe *I* killed her?"

"They want to ask you more questions," Mrs. Hua whispered. "They say to go with them."

"They're arresting me?"

"No, no," she said soothingly. "Just questions, that is all."

When she started to follow Janet to the jeep, the soldier barked two syllables at her and she stopped. "I will do my best for you." Her smile was back in place, kind and sincere. Then she gave her little giggle.

Janet remembered the giggle, coming from behind the closed door in the Foreign Students Building. "You were there," she whispered. "You were in the office with Mrs. Li that night."

The smile never left Mrs. Hua's face. "What are you saying?" she asked, honestly perplexed. Such an open, kindly face!

"When I was on my way out to meet the students on Thursday night, you were in the office with Mrs. Li."

"You are mistaken, Dr. Aldane. I was at home that night. With my sons."

"I heard you." She still whispered, not wanting to wake everyone. Her heart pounded with fear.

Mrs. Hua's eyes slid to the officer, who stood there stolidly as if he understood not a word of what they were saying. Janet stared from one to the other, unable to break through the feeling of powerlessness that overwhelmed her. Now she thought the others could hear the pounding of her heart.

The red star on the side of the jeep pulsed in time with her heart. It was suddenly huge, and symbolic of all the nameless horrors Americans had been indoctrinated with for generations. The officer stayed behind with Mrs. Hua, who stood smiling up at him. No one spoke on the short trip.

She was brought to a room with the usual cement floor furnished with two desks facing each other and bars on the windows. The two soldiers motioned to the wooden chair beside one of the desks and left, locking the door behind them. A wave of panic surged over her and she felt again the claustrophobia she had suffered as a young girl. She tried to relax and breathe deeply, but the sweat came out on her forehead and the room felt close and airless. She could hear her breath very loud in her ears.

Then the lock clicked and they were back with a third soldier. "You will ask questions. I am translate." His broad *a*'s revealed the British influence on English education in China. He stood facing her with one man at right angles to him, the other PLA man behind her. This was going to drive her batty: not only a translator who couldn't translate, but she had to look up at them and keep wondering what the guy behind her was doing. The real fear of being caught up in an alien and dangerous machinery compounded the remembered anxiety. She tried frantically to control her fingers that tore at each other and her eyes that darted around the room searching desperately for a way out.

The soldier spoke and she was jerked back to attention. The translator said, "You would like tea?"

The incongruity of the prosaic cordiality paralyzed her. She managed to nod, hoping tea would postpone the ordeal. Anyway, her teeth were chattering. Something hot would help. She hoped they weren't going to be ceremonious and bring the flower tea that was used on special occasions. To her it was like drinking perfume. Right now, if she took a sip of it she would throw up.

They brought *hong cha*—red tea—in a lidded china cup. The soldier dipped up a teaspoon of the tea and fed it to her, the way Chinese hosts used their own chopsticks to serve guests choice bits of food. No . . . not exactly that way . . . The steam that rose as he put it to her mouth felt good. The driver said something again and the translator turned to her. He looked very nervous. "You here. Not bad."

She looked up at him, puzzled. "I don't understand. *Bu dong,*" she said to the driver. *"Bu dong."* She felt elated at knowing the Chinese words, but nobody noticed.

He spoke again and the translator looked even more nervous. "You prison. Not bad. Wait here. They come."

She felt the familiar pain in her head that Mr. Therefore always brought on. "Who come?" she asked. "I want the American ambassador. I have the right to make a phone call."

It sounded crazy, even to her own ears. Prisoners had no such rights here. Firm assertiveness had got her through a number of bureaucratic obstacles since she had arrived, but somebody had to understand what she was saying before it could work. This poor soul had almost no English. No wonder he looked so nervous! It wasn't *her* plight that was putting him in a dither; it was his own.

He tried again. "You wait. Not bad."

"All right," she said in a burlesque of graciousness. "Since you ask so nicely, I'll wait. Thank you for the invitation." She gritted her teeth.

The translator breathed a sigh of relief and smiled back at her. He spoke to the driver, who nodded. Then everyone waited while she sipped her tea.

When she had finished, they urged her to her feet. "You come." He sounded as if he were coaxing her to come into dinner.

"Where are we going?"

"Prison." He smiled.

Suddenly she was sitting on the thin pallet of the bed and looking across the seven or eight feet of stone floor to the amiably vacant face that gazed back at her. She had discounted as senseless rumor that the prisons were staffed by retarded people, but the woman on the other bed in her cell was certainly not altogether with it. Why, she thought, am I assuming that she's a member of the staff and not a prisoner like myself? She *is* locked up here with me. She puzzled about it for a moment, until she realized that the other woman had not been in the cell when they had brought her. She had shuffled in from another corridor, following the soldiers and their prisoner into the cell, and then had shut the cell door behind them. The woman was here to guard her, perhaps to see that she did herself no harm. Somehow, Janet did not find this thought reassuring.

Cold seemed to rise from the cement floor—or come in through the bars. Where was her electric heater that Mr. Xu had set up for her? With dismay she saw that the only toilet she would be able to use was the white pot near the bed. She felt the fury rise in her, fighting with the tears that were welling up.

"Fuck 'em!" She gritted her teeth and damned them to hell. "I won't give them the satisfaction of crying. They can't keep me here for long. I haven't done anything illegal even by their standard of what passes for law." The agreeably interested look on the woman's face made her realize she was talking aloud. She wrapped her brocade quilt more closely around herself and settled down to wait for friends, for the American consul, for someone to come and demand her release. Thank heaven she had left her name at the embassy!

Would Mrs. Hua let them know, or would she be very careful to keep her whereabouts from them? That woman was hiding something. Whether he acknowledged it or not, the officer had heard the interchange between them and if he wasn't completely dishonest he would investigate the helpful Mrs. Hua.

A pinpoint of rationality shone somewhere in the worry. That officer was an intelligent, literate man. It was not possible that he would ignore all the motives people had for murdering Mrs. Li. But who knew what pressures he was under to solve the crime? Who knew if this was not a good time to raise an international brouhaha over another example of Western decadence and kick someone out of the country? Is that all they would do to her—kick her out? They wouldn't try her and send her to jail, would they? Or . . . even . . . *execute* . . .

It was all too much . . . too much . . . She put her head in her hands and closed her eyes.

Footsteps coming up the corridor. Looking up dully, she saw the officer, but she felt too hopeless and tired to get to her feet. Jiao Zhong En was with him.

"Janet." His voice was low. The look on his face was anguished. "Oh, my dear, I am sorry. I am so sorry."

"Zhong En, why are you here? Have they arrested you too?"

"No, they brought me to see you. They say I killed her."

"Then why am *I* here? Call the American embassy. Maybe they can get me out." It was no use. The only way out was to wake from this nightmare.

"Perhaps now you will tell us the truth, Jiao Zhong En," the officer in charge of the investigation said. "Tell us the truth or your lover will be executed."

"I have told you all I know. I know nothing of my wife's death."

"You killed her. If you do not confess, the foreigner will suffer the consequences."

"It's no use, Zhong En. It was Mrs. Hua, but they'll never believe us!"

Suddenly Mrs. Hua was there, smiling. "Oh, Dr. Aldane. You should not have done it. It is not right that you influence a good Chinese man with your Western decadence."

"Mrs. Hua, you speak English. How could you believe that I would do such a thing?"

"It is my duty." She smiled. "And Laura is my cousin."

"Laura did it! Mrs. Li destroyed her dream of China! Laura did it!"

2

"It's Laura, Janet! It's Laura! Open up!"

Groggy, her head aching, she lunged for the door and almost fell. She caught the doorknob and pulled, then remembered, fumbled with the key until she was able to turn it. "Laura!"

She came in and plumped down. "You were dead to the world."

"Oooh, don't say dead. Boy, what a dream I've been having! What are you doing here? What time is it?"

"Four o'clock. I stopped by to pay my respects to my cousin. It's either visit her here at work where I can get away fast or go to her house and be stuck there for hours. If I don't see her for a couple of days, she gets word to all the relatives. It's worse than living at home."

"Mind if I go along with you? I dozed off just before you came in and had an awful dream about being arrested for the murder. What crazy fears we carry around inside our heads!"

"Oh, please come. If you're there, she won't get at me about where I've been and the hours I keep."

"Uh. I should never sleep during the day. I feel awful."

They found Mrs. Hua in the office she shared with two other faculty members, poring over a Chinese-French dictionary. She looked tired. The hair she wore pinned back indifferently into some kind of roll was coming loose in strands and her face was haggard. But when she looked up and saw Laura and Janet, she gave her usual welcoming smile and rose. "Dr. Aldane! It is good to see you. Do you want me for something?"

"No, I just came by with Laura."

"Hello," Laura said. "Are you well?"

"Yes, I am fine. Is everything all right?"

"Yes. I just wanted to look in and say hello."

"I hear congratulations are in order, Mrs. Hua. I'm told that Luo Geng passed the examination, and Fa Ping too."

"Oh yes." She managed to look very pleased and a little nervous at the same time. "They have passed. Now Luo Geng will go to study in the United States. Perhaps he will see you there."

"If I can be of help to him in any way, you must let me know."

"Ah, thank you, Dr. Aldane. He must write letters to universities. You will read them to see that they are correct?"

"Yes, I'll be happy to do that. But I'm sure you could tell him exactly what to write and how to write it. Your English is as good as mine."

"No, no. It is not so good."

"You taught Luo Geng English, and it's excellent. How else could he pass the examination?"

"He studies very hard. He does well in the examination."

"And Fa Ping. He must have studied hard too."

"Fa Ping, he will go to France."

Neat sidestep, Janet thought. Laura looked at her cousin and bit her lip. Janet saw Mrs. Hua's eyes slide uncomfortably away from Laura's. Had he done well in the exam, or had Mrs. Hua made contact with someone at the ministry to grade his exam personally?

In her sweet and helpful way, she had been of service to many people, translating letters, writing speeches of welcome to visiting officials, even—it was rumored—managing to collect foreign currency so that favored items might be purchased. Janet remembered how she had offered to take Colette to a Chinese tailor to have some dresses made. "I will bring the dresses to you when they are finished," she had offered.

"But I must put them on to be sure they fit."

"Do not worry. If they do not fit, I will bring them back to the tailor."

It had seemed a cumbersome and inconvenient arrangement, but finally Colette had acquiesced. She had given Mrs. Hua the special currency foreigners were issued for purchases in China. Mrs. Hua had probably kept the foreign currency and paid the tailor in Chinese money. Had she used some of it to assure that her younger son would pass the French examination?

Laura's extreme reaction to the news of the murder of Mrs. Li— had she known of some kind of altercation between Mrs. Li and her cousin about Mrs. Hua's contacts with ministry officials? Had Mrs. Li threatened to expose back-door diddling with the exams?

"You're so different from Mrs. Li," Janet observed casually. "Two women of the same generation, who have been through most of the same hardships, and yet your views were so different."

Laura looked startled, and Mrs. Hua giggled. "I am not so old as Mrs. Li."

"No, but the difference in your ages was not so great as the difference in your lives."

"She believed in the revolution and I, too, believe in the revolution."

"Yes, of course. But you do so much for your children. You care about their education. I think you would do anything for them."

"Yes." The agreement was defiant.

"Did you ever talk with her about your differences?"

"She told me my sons would be useless. She said they should go to the country and work with the peasants. That they had much to learn that was not in the books. She was an ignorant woman."

Laura's jaw dropped. She had never heard her cousin speak that way about anyone.

"Did you have an argument with her about this?"

"No, she says what she pleases. I listen and say nothing."

"That takes a great deal of self-control. I wish I were that way."

"Hua Shi Ning is a very calm person. She never loses her temper," Laura said emphatically.

The three women smiled politely at each other.

"I must go," said Laura. "It's late."

"Oh, so soon? Come home with me."

"I can't today. Maybe next week."

"Yes, next week."

They said their goodbyes and Janet walked out with Laura.

3

"You know," Janet said when they were walking to the bicycle shed, "your behavior is making me suspicious."

"What the hell do you mean, suspicious?"

Janet's eyes opened wide. Laura didn't use such language—at least not when she was in China. "Well, you act as if you think Mrs. Hua has committed a crime, and that's making *me* think she has. It could give the police ideas too."

"That's ridiculous!" Laura almost shouted. Then: "Have the police said anything to you?"

"About what?"

"About Mrs. Hua. Do they sus . . . Oh, that's ridiculous!" she exclaimed again.

"What is it you think she did?"

"Nothing! Nothing at all!"

"*Did* she have a fight with Mrs. Li?"

"No! You heard her. She doesn't fight. And that's the truth."

"How did Fa Ping get through the French exam?"

"Wh . . . ?"

"We both know his French is not very good."

"Please! I don't want to talk about it."

"Relax, Laura. Having friends in high places is not the same thing as murder, you know."

"Oh, Janet. *You* don't think she murdered the old bitch? *You* don't believe that, do you?" She clutched the older woman's arm. Janet was sure she'd be able to count the nail marks later.

"Ow! Laura, let go! I doubt she was killed by your cousin."

Laura drew a deep breath. "Oh God, I've been so worried!"

And now you're not? Janet thought. What is this faith all these people have in me? In her quiet, smiling way Mrs. Hua is one ambitious mother lion. She *might* kill if her cub were threatened. "Why did you think she did it?"

"I didn't really. I was just afraid. I knew she was trying to pull strings for Fa Ping. He's a bright boy, but no matter how much she drove him, she could never make him study the way Luo Geng did. And he doesn't want to go to France. He wants to be a tourist guide, and that really kills my cousin. She thinks that kind of job is for people who aren't very bright, like Mr. Guo."

"You think she got someone in the ministry to pass him?"

"I don't know. I just know she's been trying for a long time."

"And Mrs. Li found out?"

"There are no secrets in China. Everybody finds out about everything. People just keep talking here and everything comes out eventually."

"Did Mrs. Li threaten your cousin?"

"Not really. She told her she thought it was wrong, and that she should stop. And what my cousin said—that her sons were useless."

"And Mrs. Hua said nothing?"

"Oh, she denied the whole thing, tried to laugh it off. You know how she laughs."

"Maybe Fa Ping did pass. Maybe he just managed to get through on his own. His reading and writing are probably better than his oral French. And there was no oral exam."

"Do you think so?" Laura looked at her hopefully. "Oh, I hope that's true."

"Of course, that in itself wouldn't get your cousin off the hook. If Mrs. Li threatened her and she was really scared, she might have killed her. But I don't think she did, for a pretty obvious reason. She's just too small and delicate. Mrs. Li was small too, but she was a strong, wiry woman. Mrs. Hua could never have stood face to face with her and overpowered her. She just doesn't have the physical strength."

"Oh God! That's true! She couldn't have done it!"

I hope God is right, Janet thought.

4

As Laura was getting on her bike, they saw Guo and his wife coming through the gate.

"You know Mr. Guo, don't you, Laura?"

"Yes. He was assigned to plan sightseeing trips for me when I came here to teach. I had a time convincing him to speak Chinese to me. I couldn't understand him when he spoke English."

"Isn't it awful? I'm so sorry for him."

Yue Zhen was carrying the baby. Husband and wife weren't speaking to each other, just plodding along side by side. They stopped when they saw the two Americans.

"How are you?" Laura said in Chinese.

"Hello," said Mr. Guo. "Where are you going?"

"How's the baby feeling today?" Janet asked.

"He is fine." Yue Zhen gave a small smile, but she didn't look well herself. The baby was asleep in her arms. Janet touched his cheek with one finger. His face felt cool and he slept peacefully.

"See, I told you he would be all right. Children have these things all the time. They recover quickly."

Laura bent to the baby and cooed at him. "He's a beautiful baby. My sister who lives in Buffalo, New York, just had a baby. I'm sorry I won't get to see him until I get back. I'm an aunt for the first time."

"Aunt." Mr. Guo repeated the word thoughtfully. *"Tante.* Soon," he said, "no *tantes* in China."

"That's right, isn't it? If families have only one child, there won't be any aunts or uncles. I'm glad I got in under the line in the United States."

"Some have no child." It sounded eerie, like a non sequitur pronouncement of doom. He wasn't looking at them; his eyes focused off into the distance as if he were seeing things they were not privy to.

"Well, *you* have a lovely child." Janet's heartiness was awkward. She looked at Yue Zhen and Laura; they both looked uncomfortable. Talk about obsessions! The man obviously needed help.

"He is afraid about the baby." Yue Zhen's voice was full of despair.

"The baby's fine. Don't you start worrying too." Some therapy. The "buck up, things will be fine, don't worry" school of psychology.

"I also think about operation. I will never have another child." Guo spoke automatically, with his eyes still off in the distance.

"You feel so strongly about this, Mr. Guo. Why did you agree to your wife's operation?"

Slowly his eyes came back to them.

"Laura, will you ask him the question in Chinese? Please," as Laura looked reluctant. "It's important."

Why was it important? Only her curiosity about a person's reaction to his own irrevocable decision. Young people in the United States were making such decisions these days and she wanted to know more about the consequences of deciding never to have children—or never to have any more.

"What was the operation?" asked Laura. "Sterilization?"

"Yes. You told me, didn't you, Yue Zhen, that he had agreed to let you have it?"

Yue Zhen looked suddenly confused. "Yes," she said. "No, no. I do not think so."

Janet felt she had got into something she had no business being in, but she persisted. "He didn't want you to have the operation?"

She shook her head and tears filled her eyes.

Mr. Guo was beginning to understand the conversation. "I do not know operation."

"Yue Zhen, you had the operation when your husband was away? He knew nothing about it?"

She was crying now, and Janet took the baby from her. Her husband was staring into the distance again, his head high. He gave no sign that he knew his wife was crying.

Laura said something to Guo in Chinese and he answered quickly. His neck got even stiffer, if that were possible. "I asked him if he didn't agree with the Central Committee that each family should have only one child. He told me that he is a good worker, loyal to China, and he does what must be done to save the revolution."

"We must go," he said to his wife, and took the baby from Janet.

Just then Zhong En came up and asked how the baby was, and he and Yue Zhen continued their conversation in Chinese. Then he translated for Janet. "She says the baby is fine now, but her husband does not want to leave him with the aunt. He worries about him. She says he does not want her to come to the student meeting tonight, but she will come."

"I'm surprised she defies him." Janet spoke quickly and kept her voice low. "She seems such a submissive woman."

"She is not so submissive. She has her mother's strength when she needs it. She prefers not to make an issue of most things." He went on in a lower voice. "I think she's tired of hearing about his worry. She wants to get away from him for a time. She does not say this, but I think so."

"I can't blame her. He's really obsessed. I wonder if he should get some kind of professional help."

"You mean a psychiatrist? There is not much chance of that."

"What do people do when they need help?"

"Family and friends talk to them. In extreme cases, the cadre will intervene. Often it is only to tell them to get hold of themselves and remember their duty."

"Well," she conceded, "I imagine all that's about as helpful as anything else."

"You do not think professional treatment can help people who are too confused and frightened to live out their lives?"

"Oh, some people are helped a little. But mostly I think professionals are no more successful than are good friends who listen and make appropriate noises. Professionals may know a lot about human behavior, but not how to help people change their inappropriate behavior."

"You speak too quickly." Yue Zhen, who had been looking from Zhong En's face to Janet's trying to follow the conversation, finally admitted she was lost. "English is very fast. I cannot understand."

"I'm sorry, Yue Zhen. We were just talking about people who worry too much, like Mr. Guo. We were wondering who could help him."

She looked frightened. "He is fine," she said quickly. "He will see the child is fine, so he will be fine."

"Are you all right?"

"Yes. Yes. My husband fears about the child. I was the cause."

"You were the cause? Of what?"

"We must go home now," she said.

Janet watched them walk away. "What frightens her so?" she asked Jiao.

"It is better that troubles are not discussed. Talk will cause official notice, and then there is too much turmoil, too many involved. They will survive their problems, these young people. Better to leave them alone."

"I suppose so." But she remained doubtful. She had the uncomfortable feeling that Mr. Guo was nearer the breaking point than anyone realized. And his wife was feeling very guilty about something. "Did you know she had a sterilization operation last week?"

"Yes, I knew that. My wife kept trying to convince her that it was the right thing to do, but Guo was opposed to it. I learned what she had done after it was over."

"I thought Yue Zhen said that he had agreed to it. Now Mr. Guo says that he didn't know about the operation until he got back to Beijing."

He shrugged. "Perhaps she was able to convince him that it was the right thing to do."

"No," Janet said slowly. "I don't think she could ever convince him that it was the right thing to do. He's too afraid of being left childless."

"A mistake." He shook his head grimly. She watched him looking at the departing couple. He was worried about them, too. If Guo heard about the operation only when he got back, that must account for the marked increase in his anxiety about the baby's illness. No wonder Yue Zhen was feeling guilty. Janet's heart went out to them both, but she was especially sorry for Guo. That stiff neck was maintained by prodigious efforts at control.

"Do you think the marriage can survive this?" Laura asked.

"It will have to, won't it? Divorce isn't the easiest thing in the world here. Say, *you're* not contemplating marriage, are you?"

"Wh . . . why, what made you say that?"

"I also read minds," she boomed out in a sepulchral voice. "What else would you like to know about yourself?"

"Very funny. If I married anyone, he'd have to be willing to come home with me and live in Buffalo."

"Buffalo? A fate worse than death."

"Okay. New York, then. I don't think I'd be willing to spend the rest of my life in China."

"It's not easy, that's for sure, making so many changes in a country so quickly."

"Would you do it?"

Janet glanced at Zhong En and quickly away again. "I don't know. The world is getting smaller. If they had beds on passenger planes, America would be little more than a good night's sleep away. It could be exciting."

"Yeah, maybe." She looked thoughtful, then shook her head as if to clear it. "Time to go. I'm starved."

"Stay for dinner. The food's improving dramatically. No more cabbage."

"Cabbage is good for you," Laura scolded. "It has fiber."

"Ah yes, fiber. You've been reading letters from home. Reminds me of a friend of mine. When she first heard that bran was good for you, she put it on—and into—everything. Cereals, meat loaf, stews. Couldn't figure out a way to make it edible in desserts. Damn near killed her poor husband."

Both women threw their heads back and laughed aloud—like Americans. Some people passing smiled and stared.

"My friend's expecting me. And I've got a date."

"Have fun!"

They waved to each other and Janet turned back to the Foreign Students Building. Zhong En, looking a little bewildered, also left to have dinner with his friend Mr. Xu.

5

Students and workers were beginning to come out of their rooms, some carrying bowls to the common dining room, others carrying their string bags to market. How different all this was from her own university campus, yet how much at home she felt here.

As she walked into the courtyard, the PLA officer and his sidekick drove up. "We have time to walk a little before dinner." It was halfway between a question and a command. She fell in beside him.

"You haven't got new evidence that points definitely to the killer, have you? Is that why you're here?"

"No, there is no evidence. Not even a footprint in the sand. The killer will have to tell us that he did it."

"Maybe he will, when he can no longer bear the thought of what he's done. Or she."

He sighed. "How much easier it would be if there were clues: a footprint, a dropped possession, anything that would help us finish this matter."

"You know," Janet put her thoughts into words, "the most intriguing part of the puzzle has been the stabbing. Why stab a woman who is already dead?"

"Perhaps the anger is so great that one wishes to kill again and again."

"It's possible. In that case, the killer would, I think, use the same weapon. Twenty stab wounds, maybe, after the first one has already caused death. Or fifty blows with a blunt instrument after the first one has smashed in the skull. But to strangle and then to stab . . . It doesn't make sense—on the surface."

"You can think of a reasonable explanation?"

"Well, if someone has already killed and another person wants to share the guilt—or the responsibility."

"Ah. To say, 'You must not betray yourself. If you do, you betray me also.' "

"That might be said to someone who was weak, who might kill and then confess what he has done."

"Said by someone who cared very much for him—and was very strong."

They both thought of the people involved, matching the solution with the personalities.

"Did Laura Qian love her cousin so much, do you think?"

"Laura? Oh, I don't think so. She has a great sense of family but I doubt that it extends to that kind of sacrifice. Anyhow, I don't think Mrs. Hua has the physical strength to strangle someone like Mrs. Li."

"Then what of Mrs. Hua? Is *her* love of family so strong as to cause her to share responsibility for a killing she did not do?"

"She loves her sons all right. I think she'd do anything for them. But her cousin? Someone she's known for only two years? And someone, too, who does nothing but distress her by her unconventional behavior? No. Mrs. Hua loves those who do as she tells them to do. Her sons are very obedient."

"You do not approve of obedience to parents?"

"I think adults ought to make their own decisions," she said shortly, tired of pontificating about her social views. Fretful, also, because her bits of analysis were beginning to fall into place. "Laura had no overwhelming reason to kill Mrs. Li. She wanted to live here and Mrs. Li made it impossible, but that's hardly a reason for a healthy, well-balanced young woman to kill. It's true, she's been very disappointed in China. She hasn't been as happy here as she thought she would be."

"She does not like China?"

"She had some romantic idea of coming back to the home of her ancestors and being welcomed as the prodigal daughter. But no one was overjoyed to see her, and they certainly didn't make her feel at home."

"She is very angry."

"She's hurt. She's met a young man, and for a while this will be enough. But I think she'll be going home soon—back to America. That will be her response to her anger and frustration here. Basically she's a very sensible young woman."

"Sensible because she no longer likes China?" It rankled.

"No, sensible because she knows when to give up on a dream."

"Perhaps she will come to understand one day. We have had a long history with foreigners."

"Perhaps." Janet was noncommittal. Explaining prejudice by pointing to history was justifiable. But she would not accept any defense of prejudice.

"So it was not Laura Qian. Convince me that it was also not Mrs. Hua. If she is not strong enough, perhaps one of her sons . . ."

"No." She was definite about that. "No circumstance would ever persuade Mrs. Hua to put the lives of her sons in danger. She would sooner die herself. Her whole life has been devoted to protecting them. All her commitment to duty, her self-abasement, her excessive helpfulness to those in authority—all are designed to provide a setting in which her sons will be given, if not favored treatment, at least all possible legitimate assistance."

"Her younger son passed the French examination. He has not been a very good French student."

"You know about that? I suppose she may have tried to use her influence to . . . er . . . Mrs. Li may have threatened her with exposure. Was she here the night of the murder—she and her elder son, Luo Geng? I don't remember seeing her."

"Yes. She told us they were here."

"She would never have permitted Luo Geng to be involved. Even to tell him that Mrs. Li threatened her would be to involve him."

"It is possible that her younger son may have passed the examination honestly, even though not well. There are very few French students these days. Most young people study English. The ministry may have needed three or four people to go to France for political reasons."

"And they just took those with the top three or four scores. Yes, that could be. Can you check the other passing scores and see how close they are to Fa Ping's?"

"We can do that."

"Zhong En and Xu have been very close friends for a long time." She looked at the man beside her, waiting for his reaction. When he said nothing, she went on. Was she speaking a little too quickly, too eager to absolve her friends—absolve Jiao Zhong En? She slowed down deliberately, trying to present her argument with cool deliberation. "This kind of act—stabbing someone who has already been murdered in order to assume part of the responsibility—requires, I think, two people who are dependent on each other." The word "symbiosis" came to her, but she doubted it was in the officer's vocabulary. "I think the two people would have to be everything to each other—their world in each other. Mr. Xu has two children who are very important to him; they are his world. He has his needs and responsibilities quite apart from his friend's."

"We have determined how Xu spent the evening of the murder. He bought food for his family's dinner, then he went to bathe. He was seen."

"Well." Janet sighed and smiled a little. "If Mr. Xu couldn't have killed Mrs. Li—or stabbed her—then Professor Jiao could not. Who else among the suspects would share such responsibility with him?"

He returned her smile—knowingly—and she went on: "There are only two people who could possibly have done this. I'm sure of it. But the proof—that's another problem."

6

They had circled the courtyard several times and come to the entrance of the building again. When she came into the dining room and sat with the officer, the table where all the others were already seated grew quiet for a moment. Then they began to eat and to speak again but their voices were subdued. One by one they finished and left.

Yanmin, still looking as if she would burst into tears if anyone spoke to her, came out of the kitchen to ask what she could get them for dinner. It did not seem as if her life would be changing much, no matter what had been discovered about her parentage.

"The meals are more to your liking now?"

The question brought Janet's attention back to the man who sat facing her. He was not going to ask her who had killed Mr. Li. And as sure as she was, she was reluctant to say the names. It was a terrible responsibility and she hated to take the final step. So she went along with him and made polite conversation for a while. "Yes. At last I'm beginning to enjoy Chinese food as much as I did in the United States."

"You like Chinese food?"

"I love it!"

That pleased him. Chinese people were inordinately fond of hearing that foreigners liked their food, their temples, their country. Even a man like this soldier was not impervious to what were perceived as evidences of goodwill.

Yanmin came back with a tray full of small dishes, each one piled with something interesting: pork fried and crackly in one, lotus hearts dipped in batter and fried in another, *bou cai* (cabbage), spinach, *doufou* (soybean curd), rice. And a large plateful of sliced tomatoes, unfortunately with sugar on them. Everything was delicious. The woman who had spent all her time dishing out food she was ashamed of could really cook. It was going to be a good year—unless some bureaucrat decided to replace her for obscure reasons of his own.

As Yanmin served, Janet asked the officer to ask her how she was feeling, and if there was anything that Janet could do for her. She answered that she was fine, that she needed nothing. She spoke again, and when she paused for breath, Janet asked the officer to translate what she had said. "She says that Mrs. Li's family is very good to her."

"She doesn't call her Mother?"

He shook his head. "She says she loves them all and they care for her. They have always been kind to her."

The girl said something else and Janet saw the soldier's face tighten. He asked a question and she answered.

"What is it?" asked Janet. "Has she remembered something important?"

The officer didn't answer, only listened intently. When she had finished talking, he gave her an order and she scuttled back to the kitchen, looking frightened.

"What?" Janet demanded.

"The girl is a fool," he said impatiently.

"What did she tell you?"

"She could have helped us solve her mother's murder two weeks ago."

Janet held her breath, waiting. Was this the evidence that would corroborate her solution—or would someone else be identified as the murderer?

Someone approached the table and the officer looked up and glowered. Janet couldn't take her eyes from his face. Zhong En's voice broke through to her and she felt a clutch at her heart. Was his appearance at this moment an omen?

He was apparently taken aback at the way both of them were glaring at him and he began to apologize. "I hope you do not mind that I am here."

"Do *you* have something to say that you have not said before? Something that you did not think was important?"

"No," Zhong En answered slowly. "I have told you everything I know."

"What did she tell you?" Janet broke in.

The officer took a deep breath and closed his eyes for a moment, and shook his head. "The girl saw Guo and his wife coming from the building site a few minutes after five o'clock. After the time you spoke to your wife there," he told Zhong En.

"Didn't Mr. Guo say that he was away all week visiting his sick father?"

"We know he returned on Thursday. It was a stupid lie. It was very easy for us to discover the dates on his permission to travel from Beijing."

"Of course," Janet said softly. "They were both back there."

"She was looking for Mrs. Li, who had promised to take her to a film. Dinner was almost finished and she was afraid they would be late. And because Guo and his wife are always so good and kind to her," he added sarcastically, "they said they would take her to the film the next day. They told her Mrs. Li was not to be found, that she was probably off somewhere at a meeting."

"And she never connected their presence with the murder of Mrs. Li."

"No. You see, they were always so kind to her." He shook his head in disbelief.

"She is a simple young woman," Zhong En protested. "To her, people are what they seem."

"She worried that Mrs. Li would look for her if she went home without seeing her. Yue Zhen told her that they would see the old woman later that evening, that she was coming to their house."

"Did they tell you that Mrs. Li *did* come to their house that night?" Janet asked.

"No. They said nothing about that. Only Yue Zhen says what her husband says—that he was away on Thursday."

There was silence for a while, each involved with images too undefined for sharing. Finally, Janet asked the officer, "Will you talk to them about this now?"

"Yes. At once, before they learn what we have discovered."

"I'd like to be with you when you see them."

"Yes, you may come. You, too, Jiao Zhong En. You must be there too."

It sounded ominous.

7

They rose to go. Sally was standing in the doorway staring into the twilight. The days were getting shorter. Already it was difficult to distinguish faces in the courtyard. The white shirts of the men and woman moved about with vaguely defined appendages. It was cool after the dining room. As they stood there in front of the building, from the open office window they all heard the sounds of voices coming plainly to them. Although there was no shouting or even much anger in the sounds, it was clear that the two people were arguing. They couldn't have known how their voices carried out of the open window and across the court.

Wang Qu Qing had come up and they all stood and listened. "That is Comrade Guo and his wife, Yue Zhen," he announced. "You have heard, Professor. Guo is also very angry to Comrade Li. He says she is honored woman but he very angry to her."

"Who told you this?"

"You have heard. You know."

"No, I didn't know."

"In office. I am outside. I hear. You hear also. You are outside."

"When was this? When did you hear him?"

"A long time ago. One day."

"What was he angry about? Did you hear what he was saying to her?"

"You know."

"Qu Qing, even if I heard them fighting I wouldn't understand what they were saying." Unless they were actually screaming at each other it wouldn't sound like a fight to her. She was sure that no matter how agitated Mr. Guo might become he would never scream at anyone. And Mrs. Li's most ordinary conversation sounded a little hysterical. Janet would have ignored it if she had heard her.

"He says she does not care that his child is ill. He says he will grow old and die without a son."

"What did she say to that?"

"She tells him he is not a good communist. She says she will denounce him to the committee."

"What else did you hear?"

"That is all. Mr. Guo has k . . . ?"

She eyed him threateningly, and he subsided.

"Oh!" Sally's mouth opened.

"What, Sally? You look as if you remember something."

"What? Oh. I do. I remember. The night of the murder. I *think* it was that night. I saw Yue Zhen."

She said nothing more.

"Where did you see her?" The PLA officer was much more patient with this foreigner than Janet felt. She could just hear him excusing her: she is very young.

"Here. She was here."

"Where here?" Janet wondered if *this* murder would be justified.

"She was looking for Mr. Therefore."

"Mr. Therefore?" The officer was puzzled.

"She means Mr. Guo." Embarrassed, Janet explained quickly the origin of the nickname.

"Yue Zhen couldn't find him, and then he was there."

"So?"

"Nothing. She found him."

"Where?"

A slight frown appeared on Sally's smooth forehead as she turned to look at Janet. The raised voice was getting through to her. "I met her right out front. She said she had looked everywhere. And then, there he was."

"Where did he come from?"

"Well, I'm not sure. But he didn't come from inside the building. I was blocking the door."

"Did he come through the gate?"

"He must have. He wasn't anywhere in the courtyard. And he didn't come across the court. I would have seen him."

"Maybe he came up the path from outside or from one of the other buildings."

"No." Qu Qing chimed in. "I was coming on the path. I saw Sally and Yue Zhen standing at the door. Then I also saw Guo."

"You didn't see where he came from?"

"No. As I was walking I met Zhu Mei and Dawang. When I looked again Guo was there with Sally and Yue Zhen."

Janet looked at the officer. "Then there's only one direction he could have come from—the building site."

The soldier nodded.

"How did you happen to remember all that now?" Janet asked Sally.

"The argument." They could still hear Guo and his wife. "I remember thinking she was going to let him have it when she found him."

"Yue Zhen? She looked angry? I've never seen her look anything but meek and vaguely frightened."

Even the argument now was distinguished by the lack of anger in the voices of either of the participants. Guo's voice was louder than usual, but it was controlled. She could visualize the rigidity of his neck that seemed to extend to his jaw and make his words and sentences clipped and emotionless. Yue Zhen's voice was characteristically low and hesitant. But it persisted. She was doing most of the talking.

"Well, it wasn't angry exactly. I don't know. She sort of looked *ready*. You know, like she'd been saving up things to say."

Janet was surprised at this evidence of Sally's perceptiveness.

"Where did they go afterward?" asked the officer.

"Back into the building, I think. I didn't notice."

"I did! I did!" Qu Qing was delighted to have something more to add to the conversation. He also was suddenly recalling what he hadn't before. "Yes, I saw! They went into the building. I could not go in because I am forbidden," he boasted. As if that ever stopped him!

8

Guo and Yue Zhen turned from each other as the door to the office opened and Zhong En, Janet, and the officer came in. Yue Zhen's last words hung in the air: *"Bu yao . . ."* Janet knew what they meant: "Do not . . ." What was she telling him that he must not do?

No one said anything for so long that Janet became uncomfortable. "Hello, Yue Zhen," she finally said. "Mr. Guo." The words fell on the dead silence.

Zhong En walked toward his stepdaughter and son-in-law. "The officer wishes to speak with you. He . . ."

The officer said something sharply and Zhong En stopped in his tracks. Janet could feel her heart beginning to pound and her breath sounded loud in her throat. This was going to be a dreadful confrontation.

"You lied to the police!" the officer almost shouted at Guo, as if he had just discovered the lie. "You were here on the day your wife's mother was killed!"

Janet was startled to hear the whispered translation in her ear by Qu Qing, who had followed them in. No one seemed to mind.

Guo started to say something but his wife interrupted. "No," she said. "He was in Shanxi with his father."

The look the officer gave her was freezing but she seemed not to notice.

"My husband was not here. He told the truth."

"He was seen after five o'clock, when your mother was killed."

"No. She was not killed then. She came to my house later—much later."

"You saw her after five-thirty?"

"Yes." Her voice was low but defiant. She looked the soldier right in the eye.

"You are lying too. The cook saw your mother dead at that time. There can be no mistake about that."

"*He* lied. My mother . . ."

"No." He stopped her. "There is nothing to say."

"Then we will say nothing." She tried to look at her husband warningly, but his eyes were staring at the wall behind the PLA man, as if he had not heard.

He's making a mistake, Janet thought as she listened to the exchange. He shouldn't be threatening her; she's resilient. She'll stand up to him, softly but unbreakably. Guo is the one he should be tackling; he's at the breaking point. "Mr. Guo," Janet said quietly, with confident authority. "You killed her. I know."

The face of the officer was suddenly blank. Slowly Guo's head turned from his contemplation of the wall and he saw the foreign professor.

"I know you killed Comrade Li," she said again.

His mouth opened to speak and Yue Zhen moved convulsively. Zhong En put his hand on her arm to restrain her.

"Yes," said Guo.

Janet's eyes darted briefly to the officer, but he gave no sign.

"I am the one!" Yue Zhen pulled her arm from her stepfather's grasp. "I am the guilty one!"

Janet continued as if she had not spoken. "Ever since your baby was born she was after your wife to have an operation so there would be no more children."

"She was honored cadre. Evil. *Elle veut me perdre.*"

"Yes, she wished to destroy you by leaving you without an heir."

"My family finished. No son. My name finished."

"Our son is at home," Yue Zhen said with great intensity, trying to distract him, to stop his automatic agreement with everything that was being said to him. But he didn't hear. She was only his wife. The professor was authority.

"You couldn't make the old woman stop. Your wife was beginning to agree with her."

"Wife not obey. Soon she obey mother. Wife must obey me. I am husband. I know she not obey me."

"Your wife had the operation while you were away visiting your sick father."

A shudder went through him.

"I am to blame," his wife moaned. "I alone."

"I find her to tell. She tell me traitor. Too many people for China."

"You became very angry and you put your hands on her throat."

A frown creased his smooth forehead, as if he were trying to recall. Then he spoke calmly, although there was some confusion in his words. "She did . . . I did . . . this terrible thing." His eyes went back to the wall behind the soldier.

Yue Zhen's body spoke her dejection. "You have betrayed me," she told her husband. But he didn't hear her.

"You didn't kill her, Yue Zhen," Janet said gently.

"I put the knife into her body," she almost whispered.

"She was already dead. You only wanted to save your husband, to share his guilt."

"It was my guilt. I should not have operation."

"You thought if you . . . uh . . . used the knife it would prevent Guo from going to the police? You were afraid he would tell what he had done?"

"Yes. I believe he says nothing if he is afraid for me."

"Were you there when it happened?"

"After I tell him about operation he runs from house. I know he goes to find my mother. When I find my husband he tells me what he does. I run to kitchen for knife. I am not seen."

"You went in the side door?"

"Yes, I go around front of building to other side. People come and go in kitchen."

"Did anyone look at you or say anything to you?"

"No. All busy. Guo goes with me to back. I see my mother on ground. I . . . I . . . ."

"Did you do anything else?"

"The sand . . . I take away marks. We go home. Yanmin . . . We go home."

9

Guo and Yue Zhen had been taken back to their home to arrange for the care of their child while they were detained. Now those who had heard the confession stood outside the Foreign Students Building. Even the PLA man looked unhappy.

"I think you were suspicious of Guo all the time," Janet said to him. "You knew very early that he lied about not being here that night."

"I knew he was not telling the truth, but I had no evidence that he had killed Li. He was a model worker. His behavior was always correct. There was no question that he respected his wife's mother; he said often that he was proud to be in her family."

"I'm sure he was sincere when he said that. He *was* proud. But he also wanted a family of his own. The private anguish didn't diminish the pride; it just, for a moment, took over. Immediately after, he was horrified at what he had done and was ready to give himself up to the authorities."

"It was his wife. She is the strong one. She prevented him," Jiao Zhong En said.

"Very effectively too. When she used the knife, he didn't know that any doctor would recognize it had gone into a dead body. To confess would be to destroy his family, lose him the child that meant everything to him. Who would take care of the baby if both he and his wife were arrested? It was hideous to contemplate. He had to protect his child."

"Now the child is lost to them both." She had never heard Zhong En sound so sad.

"Do you think he deserves that? Should he take the whole blame?" she asked the officer.

"You mean his wife should share the blame? She will. Perhaps her punishment will not be as severe, but she will not go unpunished."

"No, I didn't mean that. I think Guo was a victim." She looked at Zhong En when she said it. He hadn't wanted the murderer found. Almost, she agreed with him.

"Ah yes. In America they would pity him and send him to a hospital to be cured, yes?"

"Probably not, these days. I just can't help feeling sorry for him. His world wasted him—wasted his ability, his resources. In another time, another place, he might have been saved."

The officer made a motion of impatience with his hand. "In *this* time, in *this* place, he must be punished for such a crime."

"Yes, of course." Janet gave in. What was the use of such a discussion? It would change nothing.

"You think he was right to do what he did?" The officer saw she was dejected and he challenged her.

"No. No, I don't think any of it was right. It wasn't right to take a man already burdened by tragedy and turn him out of his job. To make him work in a language he didn't know, after he had struggled so hard to learn French. To send him to be nice to foreigners, when he had learned that being too nice to foreigners was not the way to get ahead in his unit. To force him to pretend to like foreigners, when he mistrusted them.

"He had frustration piled on frustration, fear upon fear. He had to live with more conflicts than most people do. And finally this one —a mother-in-law who everyone said was a person to be honored. He needed to do what everyone said, but he resented her for interfering with his life, for threatening to deprive him of a family. Another nemesis, like the one that had taken his first wife and child, the one he had been powerless to confront."

Colette came out and, for once, was silent when she sensed the depression that all of them were feeling. Janet thought she ought to tell her what had happened and relieve her anxiety, but she couldn't go over it all again. She would tell her later, when the others had gone. If Qu Qing didn't tell her first.

Some of the students began to arrive, and the officer left. "I think we will meet again," he told Janet.

She put out her hand and he took it. "I hope so," she said. "You promised to tell me the high scores on the French examination."

He smiled. "To finish it neatly."

"Not really." She couldn't muster up an answering smile. "Just another question to answer."

10

Zhong En stayed until she was alone again, sitting beside her on the bench. Although he did not take part in the talk, he seemed reluctant to leave—to be alone. She was glad he stayed; she wanted to ask him something.

"How did you happen to be here the day Guo took me to the Buddhist temple? Did he tell you he had arranged it?"

"No. I saw Yue Zhen. She was very worried about him, but she wouldn't say why. She told me that you were saying you had seen him here the night my wife was found. Somehow, I became afraid for you."

"You think he had something to do with the Buddha falling on me?"

"I think it was an accident. What he did, he did in blind anger, not planned. But I knew he was disturbed. I was afraid for you," he said again.

"Did you know he had killed your wife?"

"No, not surely. I knew only that there was no one who hated her so much—not even he. I could see that he was not thinking clearly but I could not believe he had done such a thing."

"Do you think Yue Zhen came to visit me so often because . . . ?" She shrugged, not finishing the thought. What did it matter if the young woman came to repeat her husband's alibi, to check on the progress of the investigation—or to protect her from what her husband might do? Who would ever really know but Yue Zhen?

Xing Qi Er—Tuesday

1

"Look who is here!" Wang Qu Qing announced himself the next evening. The students were all there. Mr. Xu had brought his daughters, the other Mrs. Li was there with her silent daughter, pushing her to say something in English.

Laura Qian came through the gate on her bike and stopped in front of them. "I came to say goodbye. I'm going back to the United States."

"Oh! I'm sorry to see you go!" Janet took her hand and held it.

"It's time I went. I miss everyone at home. I can't wait to see my family and all my friends." The look on her face wavered between sadness and elation. "I belong at home," she said. "Maybe not Buffalo, but America is my home. I know that now."

"Well, at least you came and found out for sure. For the rest of your life you won't have to wonder what it might have been like."

"Oh, the things I expected to find here! But it was all fantasy. They don't really need me here—or even want me very much. I thought they would," she added wistfully.

"And your friend? What about him?"

"I love him," she said simply. "But it isn't enough."

"Would he consider coming to the United States with you?"

"No, he's committed to China. He wants to be a part of what's happening here. *I* could be committed if they gave me half a chance. But I'd always be a foreigner here. Or"—she twisted her mouth wryly—"I'd be totally Chinese, and that's worse."

She thought she read disapproval in Janet's raised eyebrows, but it was only a question. At any rate, she hastened to explain. "I can't take the way people are treated here, the way their lives are run by bureaucrats and senseless regulations. You agree, don't you?"

"I know I couldn't live here indefinitely," Janet answered. "I wouldn't want to be Chinese at this time in the country's history. But there are very few young people here who would leave if they were given the opportunity."

"I guess I'm just too American. I don't have the patience to live this way—maybe for my whole life—just to help make things better for future generations."

Janet wondered fleetingly if she herself would stay longer than the one year for which she had contracted. Mrs. Hua had told her that morning that the head of the college wanted her to stay on. Murder or no murder . . . Apparently all the talk about her corrupting influence had gone on at the lower levels, where the decisions were not made.

Colette came running from across the court, where the African students had gathered after dinner. She threw her arms about Laura. "I am so sorry to see you leave. I, too, will be going home soon. To France. You must come to see me. How will you travel? I am planning to go by the Trans-Siberian Railway. It will be an adventure. But I must send my baggage ahead by ship; it is too much to carry on the train. You, too, must travel across China and the Soviet. And you will come to France. If you stay, I will be there, and you will stay with me. I do not have a home, but I have many friends. There will be no problem."

Laura laughed. "I'll write you, Colette. Maybe one day I will get to France."

"Oh, we must remain friends. I will write to you also."

Sally came out and added her goodbyes. The atmosphere was lighter than it had been in a long time. Even the old doorman left his cubicle and stood on the step smiling benignly. Chang chattered away with the students in what passed for English.

2

It was only when all the students had gone and the foreigners were back in their rooms that Zhong En came up the path to the Foreign Students Building, walked past the dozing old man, and knocked on Janet's door. She opened the door to him and went into his arms. Her curtains were already drawn carefully against any eyes that might pry from the darkened courtyard, and one of the two lamps had been turned off.

They both needed to be comforted, Janet thought. And she wouldn't be going home for at least a year.

About the Author

Charlotte Epstein is a former human relations professor. She is the author of ten books and several dozen articles in the area of human relations. As a social scientist for the Philadelphia police department she instituted a new method of police training in human relations. Dr. Epstein is the author of a book for police officers and nine other books for nurses, teachers, and paraprofessionals. Like her heroine, she spent a year in Peking teaching English to scientists. *Murder in China* is her Crime Club debut.